I0723946

PIN STRIPES

Pin Stripes

Whitetide Streak Book One

MARIE LONG

Pinstripes
(The Whitetide Streak, Book 1)

This book is a work of fiction. Any references to historical events, real people, or real places are used fictitiously. Other names, characters, places, and events are products of the author's imagination, and any resemblance to actual events or places or persons, living or dead, is entirely coincidental.

Copyright © 2023 by Marie Long
Published by Chikara Press

All rights reserved, including the right to reproduce, distribute, or transmit this book or portions thereof in any form whatsoever.

In accordance with the U.S. Copyright Act of 1976, the scanning, uploading, and electronic sharing of any part of this book without the permission of the publisher is unlawful piracy and theft of the author's intellectual property. If you would like to use material from the book (other than for review purposes), prior written permission must be obtained by contacting the publisher. Thank you for your support of the author's rights.

The publisher and author acknowledge the trademark status and trademark ownership of all trademarks, service marks, and word marks mentioned in this book.

Cover by Jacqueline Sweet Design

Printed in the United States of America

10 9 8 7 6 5 4 3 2 1

ISBN: 978-1-960253-01-9 (paperback)
ISBN: 978-1-960253-02-6 (eBook)

PIN STRIPES

CHAPTER 1

ONE! TWO! PUNCH! KICK!" DIESEL Reed barked at the sweat-drenched woman before him as she attacked his padded hand mitts to his rhythmic commands. Despite his sharp tone, he adored his beautiful client, Carina Parker, who stood in a perfect fighting stance, ready to lay into the mitts with a roundhouse kick.

Her face bore the look of a determined warrior as she fought to get back in shape through fitness kickboxing. Three days a week, two hours a day, Diesel gave her the intense personal training she desired. Diesel admired her hard work and dedication, but there was something else about her that intrigued him. Something deeper. He sensed that, under her self-doubt, this plus-sized woman hid a deliciously sexy edge. *How could someone like her not be happy with herself?* In the two months he'd known her, he'd kept this and other questions to himself, knowing it wasn't ethical to prod into a client's personal life.

Diesel watched her body move. Her plump belly, voluptuous breasts, and matching round ass, all of which he adored, were the most noticeable aspects of her weight. She was thicker than the average woman but hardly out of shape compared to some of his past clients. Carina was perfect. She carried the weight well and looked especially sexy in spandex, which revealed every curve. The bottom of her grey, sweat-soaked tank top was hiked up slightly, revealing a small portion of her bare, caramel-toned belly beneath.

He swallowed, his weakness for curves sending shockwaves of pleasure straight to his dick. *So what if she's a client?* He'd love to get to know her more. He'd watched her transform from a timid, self-conscious doe, who was afraid to set foot in his gym, to a sassy tigress.

A tigress… A mate…

The hand mitts yielded to another of Carina's swift, accurate punches, and he snapped out of his thoughts. They'd been going at the drill for fifteen minutes straight, and she continued pushing herself harder.

"You're doing great, Ri," he said. "Again."

Carina gritted her teeth and slammed a roundhouse kick into the left mitt. The impact moved him back an inch. *Damn.* Her strength matched her beauty—just two of the many things he loved in a woman.

Bam!

His arm flew back from the force of a powerful punch, and he started, his fantasies dissolving.

Carina huffed. "How's that?"

Fucking amazing. He grinned and lowered the mitts. "Damn, girl, I know grown men built like football players that can't hit as hard as you."

She let out an airy chuckle. "So you're saying I hit like a girl?"

"A girl? Hell no. You hit like a badass *woman!*"

"That's because I have a drill sergeant of a trainer."

"Hey, I'm not *that* bad…" He paused then his smile turned lopsided. "Unless you want me to be."

"Have I not sweated enough?" She plopped down on a nearby bench. She retrieved a water bottle from her black gym bag and tilted her head back, guzzling half its contents. A trickle of water dripped down the side of her mouth and neck then trailed down her chest, where it disappeared in her cleavage. What he wouldn't give to chase that lucky little drop of water with his tongue.

His gaze then flicked to her tank top, where the small beads of her nipples protruded. The stretchy ribbed fabric strained across the span of her captivating breasts, which jiggled and bounced with the rest of her body's movements. He drifted off in his thoughts again, to his private office in the back of the gym, where he could have Carina splayed topless across his desk while his mouth had his way with her nipples—licking her, sucking her, and teasing her until she screamed his name. His dick steeled at the fantasy. His vision blurred, and for a moment, the colors in his sight began to dull—a clear sign that losing control of his tiger was imminent. He clenched his jaw as he struggled with every ounce of his willpower to reel in the horny beast that fought to rip through his subconscious and claim this woman.

"So how much longer do you think it will take me to lose this?"

Diesel snapped his gaze back to her face. The colors in his vision returned to their vibrant hue.

Gathering himself, he felt the animal in him return to its slumber. She was looking back at him expectantly, and part of him wondered if she'd caught him staring at her breasts. "Come again?"

Giving him a look, she pinched and jiggled a handful of her belly fat. "I'm working so hard, and I still can't lose an inch. How much longer do I have to keep going through this sweaty hell?"

His attention zeroed in on the way she grabbed herself, and he swallowed, wishing she hadn't done that. Pain surged to his hardened dick, and he wished he were the one grabbing her like that. He gritted his teeth and let out a small hiss. "I can't tell you when you'll lose it," he said through the pain. *Fuck… please don't lose that sexy belly.*

Rolling her eyes, she shouldered her bag and stood from the bench. "I guess I should've known better than to ask you."

"You shouldn't be so worried about it, anyway."

Her eyebrows shot up, and she looked at him as though he were from another planet. "Are you serious, D? I'm thirty-five and still single because I had to learn the hard way that guys don't like girls with too much weight in the middle."

A low growl rumbled in his throat. He would love to meet the bastard who'd told her she had too much weight. *I would fuck him up until he's unrecognizable.* "You just haven't met the right guy," Diesel said, trying to sound as calm as possible.

"I've met enough of you so-called 'decent' guys to know your real tastes in women. Trust me. This Southern girl's had more bad luck than a mouse in a tiger's den."

Amused by her strange analogy, he fought down his smile. "Hey, don't lump *me* with the assholes you've been with."

She looked at him for a moment then laughed. *That laugh.* So contagious, so sexy. "You're right. You're nothing like them. You're my personal trainer, helping me to better myself. That's more than I can say about those other guys."

"You mean, the other *boys.* You're way too mature and sophisticated to be dealing with that."

She snorted. "'Mature'? I'm only one year older than you."

He gave her a reassuring smile. "You know what I mean." Her age didn't faze him, and she wasn't sure if her quip was intended to hint at something else.

"Sorry, D. I'm just so salty right now. I really wish I could just find someone worth spending my time with, y'know?" She took out her keys from her duffel bag.

"Yeah…" Diesel half-listened and noticed the dozens of rings, charms, and a mini stuffed tiger attached to her keyring. She liked big cats, it seemed. A good sign. Maybe he could give her something else to remind her of him. He perked up with an idea. "Hang on a sec." He rushed over to the front desk, retrieved something from behind it, and returned to Carina. Smiling, he handed her a small keyring with the Nine Stars Gym logo on it. "Here. To add to your growing keyring collection," he said.

She stared at the charm a moment, then slowly took it, chuckling. "Gee, thanks." She found a new home for the charm right next to the stuffed tiger. Afterward, she turned and started walking away. "Later, D."

He ogled her ample ass as she walked toward the women's showers. Every day she walked off like that, he'd gotten a better view as it became a little more defined from the training. She might have not yet lost the belly fat like she wanted, but she sure as hell had gained an even better ass. He'd been caught up with this woman since the day she first walked through the door of his gym, but she seemed determined to impress someone else.

He couldn't bear to see her end up with another abusive asshole. But she didn't seem to have any intentions of giving him a chance. To her, he was just her trainer, and theirs was supposed to be a mutual teacher-student relationship. But his tiger demanded a mate—demanded *her*—and the beast would stop at nothing to obtain its prize.

The women's bathroom door closed behind Carina, and Diesel once again became aware of the sights and sounds of the rest of the gym. It was four o'clock—time to get the hell out of there while the rest of his staff handled things until closing time. It was good to be the boss when he could set his own hours, and his awesome staff made the workload much easier.

Diesel was packing away his equipment in his gym bag when his cell phone buzzed in his back pocket. He started, then swiped the phone and checked the screen.

"*4:30 –Cammy,*" the popup calendar notification said.

Shit, Diesel thought, slapping his forehead. He'd completely forgotten about his younger sister arriving today. Anxiety knotted in his gut as he thought about having to deal with her for a whole week. It was her birthday, and all she wanted was to spend it with her "favorite big brother." But Diesel knew what she really wanted.

With a deep sigh, he dragged his feet out of the gym and prepared his mind for the long, agonizing week.

CHAPTER 2

Carina plopped on her bed and stared at the slow-spinning blades of her ceiling fan. She heaved a huge sigh as the sounds of the city's evening bustle outside her apartment window soothed her. After another stressful workday at Dice 'n Grill, followed by her intense personal training at Nine Stars Gym, her mind and body ached from exhaustion. She should have been used to the routine by now, but over the past week, she'd stepped up her training at the gym for some reason. Maybe it was the constant nagging thought that she hadn't met her body-image goals yet. She *had* shed some pounds, but her favorite jeans were still tight. She wanted to try the dating scene again, but it seemed like that was never going to happen at this rate.

She was thankful to have such an encouraging, helpful, and insanely sexy personal trainer like Diesel Reed to keep her motivated. She could only wonder what went through his mind every time he saw her. No doubt, he was probably completely turned off by her—guys like him usually were— but he hid those thoughts well under a charming personality.

Every time she fantasized about caressing his olive skin, feeling every muscle on his athletic frame, or running her fingers through his short dirty-blond hair, her rational side warned her not to fall for his bait. That was how she'd ended up in her previous fucked-up relationships. Diesel seemed like the perfect guy she always wanted but could never have. Getting him to see her as more than just a client was wishful thinking. Diesel didn't wear a ring, but odds were, he was taken. Hot guys like him were *always* taken.

Carina pulled herself out of bed and trudged to the kitchen to make kale soup. The light, healthy dinner to end the day would hopefully help with her weight-loss goals. The way Diesel looked at her when she mentioned her weight piqued her curiosity. His jaw had tightened when she pinched her belly fat to emphasize her point. *Damn. I must've totally grossed him out when I did that,* she thought.

Her mind continued swimming. *Then why in the hell did he say that I shouldn't be worried about my weight? Was that his way of being nice? Or does he just not give two shits about whether or not I reach my goal? Or maybe he's intentionally keeping me from reaching my goal so I have to keep paying him.* She scowled at that thought. If that ended up being the case, she would get herself another trainer.

Sitting on the kitchen counter next to the unopened mail, her cellphone suddenly beeped, its screen lighting up. While the soup simmered in the pot, Carina picked up the phone.

You have 2 new admirers! the notification banner for the Plenti of Dates app read. Grinning with anticipation, Carina opened the app and took a peek at her two new suitors. As she read their stats, her smile quickly fell. No job, no education, no car, lives with their mother, recently divorced with kids, prefers to bathe only on weekends, looking to hang out at the bar every night... Their lists of undesirable traits went on and on.

She closed the app without bothering to view their pictures. Even if they were attractive, she could never see herself spending time with a man—human or shifter—who was too lazy to take care of himself.

"Why the hell do I keep attracting these immature *boys*?" she grumbled to herself.

"You just haven't met the right guy."

Carina blinked, thinking of Diesel's earlier words. She flicked her gaze toward her keys on the counter, and the Nine Stars Gym keyring Diesel had given her earlier. Maybe he was right that she hadn't met the right guy. At this rate, she sure as hell wasn't going to find any decent guy on that stupid dating app, either.

Setting her thoughts aside, she fixed herself a bowl of soup. Her phone rang. It was the manager at Dice 'n Grill. Carina had been called off work tomorrow morning, much to her surprise. A bad sign. In the five years she'd worked at Dice 'n Grill, she'd never missed a day or been called off. But Carina always knew how to turn life's lemons into the best-tasting Southern-style lemonade.

After ending the dreaded call from her manager, Carina returned to the counter, claiming one of the barstools, and sorted through her mail while the soup cooled.

Beneath the pile, which was mostly junk mail, a white-and-gold flyer caught her eye.

"Be elegant. Be empowered. Be YOU!" the calligraphic glittery-gold headline said. The flyer's background contained a piece of lingerie wrapped around a high-heeled shoe, the discreet image leaving much to the imagination. The flyer was an advertisement for a photography studio downtown that specialized in boudoir.

Carina gave an empty laugh. *No fucking way in hell,* she thought, wrinkling her nose at the flyer. It was bad enough she got ridiculed for her weight. If she ever stepped into a photo studio, she would surely be a laughingstock. Decent lingerie was hard to find in her size, and she doubted the studio would have anything that would make her look remotely glamorous.

She'd heard about the recent trend of women—young and old, big and small—getting boudoir shots of themselves as some sort of self-confidence boost and empowerment. But the idea bewildered Carina. *There's nothing "empowering" about seeing a half-naked big girl in frilly lingerie...*

She grabbed the flyer, about to toss it in the trash with the rest of the junk mail, but paused. Staring at the shoe-and-lingerie image again, she tried to envision herself wearing them. At thirty-five, she'd never worn lingerie before—never had a reason to—and part of her wondered what it might feel like to wear a piece. Did it really as feel as good as some women say?

Sinking her teeth into her bottom lip, she reconsidered her thoughts. *Ah, what do I have to lose at this point?* She could use a good confidence boost, if boudoir really *did* live up to the hype. These photos would be for her eyes only. Maybe the studio would be able to work some apocalyptic miracles to make her look like a supermodel.

Carina conceded and dialed the contact number on the flyer. While she waited, she glanced at the clock. It was after nine thirty, and the studio was most likely closed, but she could leave a message.

Moments later, a sultry female voice answered. "Good evening. Blushing Butterfly Studio. Autumn speaking."

Carina blinked. "Ah, h-hi, Autumn. I didn't realize you were open this late."

"We're open till 11:30, sweetie," Autumn said.

"Good to know. I got one of your flyers in the mail today. I'm... um... interested in doing some boudoir shots."

"Oh? That's wonderful. Is this for a wedding? Or someone special?"

Carina swallowed a lump in her throat. *Wedding... that's totally off the table, too...* "No, just me."

"So, it *is* for someone special."

Carina opened her mouth to respond, then closed it, Autumn's comment rendering her speechless.

"Have you ever done boudoir before?" Autumn continued.

"N-No..."

"Well, I will tell you that it is a very personal—very *sacred*—affair. The moment you step into my studio, you will transform into the person you were meant to be."

Who am I meant to be? Carina thought as she mulled over the woman's words. Of course, she had wished to be thinner, if only to finally find her true love and be happy. But she doubted a photoshoot would be able to do that. "I need a lot of work," she said with a hollow laugh.

Autumn chuckled. "That's what all my new clients say. There's no job too difficult when it comes to expressing true beauty."

"I don't know about that. I can't even find lingerie my size. I'm a big girl."

"Even better. When can you come to the studio?"

Carina thought for a moment, then glanced at her thick planner that sat on the counter. She slid it closer to her, then opened it to a page decorated with washi tape and stickers, with events and bulleted lists handwritten on the ruled columns. She ran her finger down the dated columns and frowned at tomorrow's date, which was now free, thanks to the earlier call from her manager. *Lemons into lemonade...* "Is tomorrow okay?" she asked Autumn.

"Tomorrow's perfect. I'll book you for a session at nine a.m. Come as you are, and watch the magic unfold."

Is this woman for real? Carina's curiosity steamrolled over her cautious rationale. Autumn sounded confident in her work. "A-All right. I'll see you tomorrow."

"Looking forward to it," Autumn said. Carina could practically hear the smile in her voice.

Carina ended the call and stared at the number on the screen until it dimmed. She gulped her soup, her mind jumbled with thoughts and questions that she hoped would be answered soon.

CHAPTER 3

SOME THINGS NEVER CHANGE."

Diesel looked sideways toward the passenger's seat, where his kid-sister, Cammy, sat, looking back at him with her usual mischievous grin. It had been seven years since he'd last seen her, after he'd broken away from his clan, the Whitetide Streak.

And somehow, here she was again, back in his life.

But why, he wondered, was she wasting her time—wasting her birthday—coming to see him?

"What can I say?" he replied to her. "I'm a routine guy."

Cammy, the youngest, and only girl of his four blood-siblings, wasn't a cub anymore. She'd grown into a beautiful, strong woman who lived a carefree life. Golden hair done up in cute little buns, and silky-soft olive skin that complemented her fiery-orange eyes—the tiger that burned inside her. She was thin and lithe, dressed in a pair of grey cut-off shorts over black-and-white, tiger stripe-patterned leggings, and a purple crop top that showed off her tight, four-pack abs.

Everything about her was Carina's goal. And Diesel fucking hated it.

He clenched his jaw at the thought of his gorgeous plus-sized client. She was probably somewhere crying in the mirror about not seeing the results she wanted. He hated a woman who wasn't happy with herself, or a weak-minded woman who let the world sway her to conformity.

"Routine is boring," Cammy said.

Diesel snorted, focusing his eyes on the road as he continued navigating the streets toward the address that Cammy had given him. "I'm happy, that's all that matters."

"You must have a shitty sex life, then."

Diesel's breath hitched at her bold statement. She'd always been blunt with her thoughts, but she'd just taken this conversation to a whole new level. "Did you come all the way here just to nag me about my sex life?"

Cammy's smirk twisted coyly. "No, but by the sound of it, your sex life is a big, fat zero."

He bristled. "That's none of your business."

"Oh yeah?" Her gaze flicked to the console. Then she swiped up his phone from the holder.

Diesel growled. "Put that back!" He held one hand on the steering wheel and clawed at her with the other.

Cammy dodged out of the way while she scrolled through his contacts. "Do you even have a little black book of potential mates?"

"Gimme my phone, damn it!"

Cammy stopped scrolling and perked up. "Who's this?" She showed him the phone screen with a picture of Carina. It was one he'd took while she was deep into one of her weight training sessions. He remembered that day vividly. She was drenched in sweat from head to toe, and her hard nipples protruded against her tight spandex top like they always did.

"None of your fucking business!" he snapped.

Cammy looked at the picture again, and smirked. "Oh, my. It must've been cold that day."

He ground his teeth. *No, her tits are just fucking amazing.*

"So, this is her, isn't it?" Cammy continued.

Realizing his sister was not giving back his phone anytime soon, he conceded and continued driving in silence.

"Have you two mated?"

He stayed silent, biting his tongue.

"D, my favorite big brother, I had high hopes for you. Surely, by now, you would've mated. You're the level-headed one of the bunch. Why not carry on the clan in your own way? Since, y'know... you couldn't take it from Axle..."

He frowned. After battling his eldest brother for the Alpha position—and failing miserably—Diesel had decided to step away from clan duties and traditions indefinitely. He'd doubted his own abilities, which had led him to the gym. He wasn't sure if and when he would challenge Axle again—or if he even *wanted* to. Diesel desired a mate, but he didn't want to get caught up with his immediate family again. "I don't have time for that," he muttered under his breath.

Cammy snorted. "Bullshit. You need a mate." She returned the phone to its holder on the console.

He shot a glare at her. "If you're so bent on carrying on the clan, why don't *you* do it?"

"Because I don't desire a mate. I'd rather live life by my own rules, my way."

His heart sank a little as he digested her response. "Y-You'd rather be alone?"

"Yeah. And I prefer it that way. I don't want to deal with cubs, clan duties, and all that political shit. Besides, I'm not an intimate kind of person, y'know?" She waved her hand dismissively. "Meh, you wouldn't understand. Just know that I'm very happy the way I am. I just want to enjoy *me*."

He nodded slowly, trying to make sense of it. He didn't think such ideas were possible, since tigers were highly sexual creatures. At first, Diesel simply thought Cammy was going through a phase, but then he realized she was being dead serious. He'd never known a woman who had such a steeled resolve for her future. One that didn't involve kids or family. But she knew exactly what she wanted, and she was indeed happy about it.

More than he could say about Carina.

At last, they pulled up in front of a small, rustic, five-story apartment building. Diesel stared at the lighted entrance, where a sign that said 'Hostel Vacancy' hung in the window.

Cammy grabbed her duffel bag from the backseat and opened the passenger's door. "Thanks, D. See ya soon."

Diesel paused a beat. "How long are you staying here for?"

"Mmm... Probably a week or so, give or take. Maybe longer, depending on my mood."

"You mean, you don't have a train ticket back home yet?"

She laughed. "No, silly. I always go one-way. Life is unpredictable, y'know? There's nothing worth going back home to, anyway. So much in-fighting and stupid shit. I want to be as far away from it as possible." Her eyelids fluttered downward a moment. "I wish Aunt Evaline were still here. She'd be able to straighten it out like she'd always done."

The mention of their late aunt sparked mixed childhood memories. Evaline was once the matriarch of the clan, and she'd ruled with an iron claw. The Whitetide Streak was as strong and orderly as their leader. When Diesel and his siblings were cubs, she would lay into them whenever they misbehaved. After her death, however, the family had fallen into disarray and never recovered.

"What problems could they have? Axle is the Alpha. The Whitetide Streak continues through his guidance," he said.

Cammy pursed her lips and shook her head slowly. "Not really... Later, D." She proceeded out of the car and walked to the hostel's entrance without another word.

Diesel emerged from Lake Hyacinth's cool water after a long, refreshing swim under the stars. He climbed onto the floating dock and shook himself dry until his orange-brown, black-striped coat became a short, scraggly mess. Quiet, clear nights were perfect for him to let his tiger roam free, away from the temptations of losing control around others. Besides, his tiger loved the water. It was his solace, and nothing could relax him more than a good swim.

He brooded over his issues, namely his sister's visit, and the brief conversation they had earlier that evening. The way she'd prodded into his personal affairs, he wondered if she knew something more about himself than he did. Cammy was pretty observant of people and their feelings. Even as cubs, he would often confide in his little sister. She was the only one who truly listened.

Perhaps now it was time for him to do the listening this time.

"Your sex life is a big, fat zero."

Diesel clenched his jaw at Cammy's words that stung him deep. He had no sex life, but he hoped to change that real soon, now that he'd found his potential mate. Carina was his current prey. All she needed was a little nudge in his direction, then he would claim her. Thinking of claiming her in his bed, Diesel let out a satisfied growl. Once she was his, he would start a new life here in the mountains of Hunter's Rest, secluded from the world, with a family of his own.

Family... The back of his throat rumbled with a low snarl. Aside from Cammy, the family he'd once known was full of selfish, egotistical backstabbers who expected too much out of him. When he left home, he'd vowed to never follow in their footsteps.

He left the dock and padded up the narrow wooden steps leading to the back porch of his cabin. He stopped before the double French doors and concentrated, allowing his tiger to return to its slumber once more. His muscles cramped as his bestial strength receded. His fur coat was replaced with skin. The muted colors in his vision became clear and saturated in the light cast from the light fixture of the overhead patio fan, but he could no longer see distant places touched by the darkness of night. His shifting complete, he rose to his feet and ran his fingers through his wet hair. He grabbed a beach towel from the wooden rack and wrapped it around his naked waist.

Diesel headed inside and retired to his bedroom. His cell phone suddenly rang. He looked at the phone, which was face down on the night table, wondering who would be calling him so late at night. His heart fluttered at the thought of Carina finally deciding to call him. He grabbed the phone and stared at the lit-up screen. All hope was shattered when he recognized the number of one of his former clients. Clenching his jaw, he hesitated. He finally answered on the fourth ring, forcing a cheery voice. "Hey, Leah."

"Diesel! Hey! Glad I was able to finally catch you," Leah said in her usual bubbly tone. Like some of his former female clients, Leah had been training with him solely to get close to him. He'd sensed her deeper attraction to him by the way she'd deliberately flaunted her goods during training and her frequent questions about his nightly or weekend plans. Women like her were largely uninteresting. There was no challenge to their cheap thrills. Fortunately, after a few weeks of his ignoring their advances, those women moved on and found some other sucker to take their bait. Diesel had lost contact with many of them—good riddance—except for Leah, who was the most persistent. They'd ended up becoming friends, and to his relief, she'd later married a rich businessman.

Diesel had kept his distance ever since she'd happily tied the knot, but he was always there to lend her a hand whenever she needed it. He never allowed his small gestures to go any further than basic friendship.

"I've been busy," he said. "Work gets demanding when you own a gym."

"Yeah, yeah, I know the deal."

"How are you doing?"

"As well as can be. I think my little bean is ready to escape." She laughed.

He smiled slightly, and he flicked his gaze to the dresser, where a pink teddy bear wearing a matching pink ribbon around its neck sat. She'd gone through the trouble of inviting him to her baby shower—the first baby shower he'd ever been invited to—so he'd thought the least he could do was get her a gift. But he wasn't particularly excited about attending. Despite pregnant women being his weakness, the thought of celebrating a baby was a constant reminder of his lack of a mate and a family of his own.

"Everything will be all right. Have you finally decided on a name?"

"Yes, actually! Paul and I agreed on Najia."

"Cute."

"You're still coming this weekend, right? I'm doing my rounds, getting last-minute confirmations from all the guests."

"Yeah, I'll be there. How many people are you expecting?"

"Close to thirty. It's going to be a fun shower! And the restaurant I booked has the best Italian food in town. I can't wait to see you again!"

He cringed. Her tone sounded a little too enthusiastic for his mood. "Well, I'm sure you and Paul will be busy with the party."

She paused. "Right. I take it you're still single."

He lifted an eyebrow, her matter-of-fact tone catching him off guard. "And what if I am?"

She laughed. "Don't worry. Paul is everything I need and more. But even over the phone, I can tell that you haven't changed a bit."

"What can I say? I'm a routine guy," Diesel said flatly. Then he bit his tongue as déjà vu struck him, and Cammy's words from earlier replayed in his mind like a bad dream.

"Routine is boring."

CHAPTER 4

CARINA STOOD OUTSIDE THE IVY-COVERED brownstone and stared up at the ornate bronze sign affixed to the wall. The Blushing Butterfly Studio was discreet and easily missed for any passerby. Perhaps for good reason. She was five minutes early for her appointment, but she'd dreaded every minute of the drive here.

Me? In boudoir? she mused. *I can't do this...* She stared at the sign again and took several deep breaths. *Well, the photos would be for my eyes only, so maybe I can try...*

She trudged up the steps and entered the brownstone. Framed portraits of beautiful, lingerie-clad models decorated the tiny interior's exposed brick walls. A dark-haired woman wearing matching cat-eye glasses and a multi-colored chiffon top sat behind a mahogany desk, typing steadily on a computer. As the door slowly shut behind Carina, her slender fingers stopped and she looked up from the monitor. A warm smile graced her olive face, highlighting the faint freckles that peppered her cheeks and the bridge of her nose.

"Hi there. Do you have an appointment?" she asked.

Carina chewed her bottom lip, then nodded once. "Ah, yeah... Are you Autumn?"

The woman's smile grew. "Nah, that's my boss. I'm Katie."

"I see. Well, hi, Katie. I'm Carina. I have a nine o'clock appointment."

Katie perked up. "Oh, yeah! So, you're Carina?" She paused and gave her an appraising glance. "Autumn has been *so* excited to meet you."

Carina cringed. "Well, I hope I won't be too much of a let-down..."

"Absolutely not! Come with me." Katie stood, gave a small head gesture to Carina and headed down a short, narrow hallway.

Carina followed warily, her heart pounding. Four closed doors lined both sides of the hallway.

Katie approached the last door on the left, which had an affixed gold nameplate that said 'Main Studio.' She knocked twice, then slowly cracked the door open.

"Autumn, your nine o'clock is here," Katie announced.

A bright flash suddenly went off. Carina craned her neck and spotted the back of a white umbrella attached to a light stand.

"Excellent! Send her in. I'm just doing some equipment adjustments," a familiar sultry voice responded.

Katie opened the door all the way and stepped aside. Beaming, she ushered Carina in. "Go on. She's waiting."

Carina hesitated and sidled inside. A chill ran through her as the room's cool, crisp air whisked over her bare skin. The room was small and quaint, with lace and silk decorating everything like a set for an erotic movie. In one of the areas, which was dressed up like a bedroom, an auburn-haired, plus-sized woman wearing a green camisole and multi-colored leggings walked out from behind a camera posted on a tripod. Spotting Carina from afar, she beamed, her ruddy face glowing like the sun.

"Carina! It's so nice to meet you!" the woman greeted. "I'm Autumn."

Carina forced a small smile as she gave Autumn the once-over. It eased her a bit to see another woman her size. Maybe Autumn would know how to work miracles and make her beautiful. "H-Hi, Autumn," she said at last.

"First of all, don't be shy. For the next three hours, this is your palace. And when you walk out that door, you will forever be a queen."

Carina scrunched her nose. "You probably say that to all your clients."

Autumn's bubbly expression morphed into amusement. Thin streams of white smoke exhaled from her nostrils. "I do, actually," she replied. "And you know what? I really mean what I say. I'm not in the business of bullshitting people. Photography is an art, and I am an artist, as we dragons naturally are. When a woman tells me they are not beautiful, I always prove them wrong. Art never lies."

Carina opened her mouth, then closed it. Straight and to the point, this woman was. Like most dragons were. Carina sort of liked it. Maybe there was hope. There was only one way to find out.

Autumn walked around Carina, studying her from top to bottom. Then she nodded thoughtfully and said, "Okay, we're going to get started right away. First, clothes, hair and makeup. I have an award-winning cosmetology staff ready to work their magic on you." She pointed toward a door at the opposite end of the room that said 'Prep Room' on a gold nameplate. "Once you're done in there, it'll be photoshoot time!"

Carina furrowed her brow. "What kind of clothes do you have for me?"

Autumn beamed. "I have an entire closetful of clothing for you. Choose only one. That is all you will need. My prep team will direct you."

"Um... are you... are you sure you have something in my... size?"

Autumn raised her eyebrows in amusement. "Honey, I am always prepared. Now, come." She spun and headed toward the Prep Room.

Carina stood speechless for a moment, then followed. Autumn opened the door, revealing three women standing around the hair station, chatting. The door closed behind Carina and Autumn, and the three women paused and looked up.

"What'll it be today, Mistress?" the blonde asked. She wore a black apron and a gold nametag that read "Emma – Nail Technician."

Autumn patted Carina's shoulder. "Have our new queen ready in an hour. And make sure she chooses a set from Armoire Number Five."

Another woman with thick, curly, dark-brown hair approached Carina and scanned her up and down. Her nametag read "Delisa – Makeup Artist." She beamed, her slit-pupiled hazel eyes flashing a soft, white hue. "*Dios mío!* Her face... *tan bonita!*" She gave a chef's kiss.

Carina forced a small smile. *I sure don't feel pretty compared to the rest of the women here.* She'd figured the overzealous makeup artist was most likely paid to say encouraging words to all of their clients to make them feel better. The thought left a bitter taste in her mouth. *This is all pretend, make-believe. When I leave this place, this will all be a dream...*

She looked back at Autumn, only to find that she was gone. The photographer must've slipped out while Carina was gawking at the prep crew. Now, she was here alone, and there was nowhere to run. *What could these three possibly do to give me the ultimate transformation?* she wondered.

"Hi, I'm Melanie. What's your favorite color?"

Carina shook out of her thoughts and looked upon the third woman standing before her. She was thick—not as thick as Carina—and tall, with flawless bronze skin that glistened in the light. Her hair was braided in perfect cornrowed extensions with orange and yellow beads at the ends. Her nametag read "Melanie – Fashion Specialist."

"Uh... I like green," Carina said at last.

Melanie's face brightened and she clapped her hands together. "Ah, the color of money. Luck. Good health. Envy..."

"And emeralds," Delisa interjected. "*Mi abuelo* collects emeralds. You should see his hoard."

Carina quirked a smile. "I own a favorite pair of emerald earrings I bought from a craft fair several years ago."

"*Ay!* You should've brought them with you! Oh, well. We will make do with what we have." Delisa winked.

Melanie took Carina's hand and led her through a doorway to another room. This room was much bigger and looked like a giant closet with wooden armoires and shelves full of neatly-stacked clothes, shoes, and accessories. Each of the armoires and shelves had numbers carved into the wood. They stopped in front of Number Five, and Melanie opened the doors.

"Take your pick, and it's yours," she said. "Complimentary with the photoshoot. Think of it as a reminder of one of the greatest days of your life—your ascension to royalty. All of these pieces are custom made by a talented seamstress—and one of our dearest cousins—who lives back in our hometown."

Carina ogled the various lingerie that came in assorted types and colors. She picked up the first one—a black, two-piece set—examined it, and blushed.

Melanie giggled. "No time to be shy. Boudoir is all about expressing a woman's power and femininity."

Carina chewed her bottom lip. Truth be told, she'd never in her life owned a set of lingerie. She had nobody to impress but herself, and the last thing she wanted was to see herself in sexy clothing and be constantly reminded about her nonexistent sex life. "I... I don't know... maybe this is a bad idea," she muttered.

Melanie raised her eyebrows. "Nonsense. You need this more than ever. Y'know, Autumn was like you once—self-conscious about her appearance, especially her weight. Then one day in college, we played a prank on her and hid all her clothes, and she was only allowed to wear the lingerie we bought her."

"That sounds like a pretty mean thing to do," Carina said.

"Yeah, but she's practically our sister, so we could mess with her like that," Melanie continued. "Besides, Delisa, Emma, and I hated seeing her sulk around and be all depressed about her appearance. So, we wanted to do something to force her to break out of that fear. We all knew she was beautiful, but we had to make her see that for herself.

"Autumn took the bait, and ended up falling in love with herself. She was so over her self-consciousness in that lingerie, she didn't want to take it off! She took picture after picture of herself in the lingerie. She got so obsessed with it, she eventually got into boudoir, and opened this studio. And the rest is history."

Carina gave a small smile. *Can a simple piece of lingerie really boost my confidence?* she wondered, reaching out to another folded piece. Her eyes then drew toward an emerald-green embroidered lace one-piece set. She unfolded it, and grimaced.

There was very little to the outfit, and she wondered just how much it would cover her. "Uh, how do I put this on?"

Melanie chuckled. "I'll help you."

It took less than ten minutes for Carina to step out of her frumpy oversized T-shirt and leggings, and step into her new outfit. To her surprise, it ended up fitting perfectly, supporting her large chest, and conforming to the extra curves of her belly, hips, ass, and thighs. It was as if this piece was made for her. And yet, as Carina stared at herself in the mirror, she felt awkward in this foreign experience.

"You look beautiful, Carina," Melanie said breathlessly.

Carina smiled back. It felt nice, and the green looked nice against her skin. *Maybe there really* is *something to this...* She thought about Autumn's first experience.

Melanie retrieved a black, velveteen robe and slipped it on over Carina's shoulders. Then she took Carina's hand and led her out the room. "Now let's get your hair in order."

Carina gulped, the thought of others seeing her dressed like this drawing anxiety in her chest. She resisted a moment, then slowly walked with her.

Carina's heart pounded as they returned to the prep room, where Emma and Delisa were. They looked her way and their eyes widened.

"*¡Dios mío!*" Delisa exclaimed.

"Ooohhh... I love it!" Emma gushed.

Heat scorched Carina's cheeks. She quickly cinched the robe around her body.

Melanie tugged Carina to the salon chair in front of her station. "Stop gawking, you two. It's time to get to work. Now, Carina, please have a seat."

Carina hesitated, staring at the pink vinyl chair as though it were booby-trapped. The back of her throat tightened. Then she spotted the scores of framed cosmetology licenses and awards posted around the lighted mirror of Melanie's station and relaxed a little.

She's a professional. She knows what she's doing, Carina told herself. *Just... trust the process.*

At last, she eased herself into the salon chair and stared back at herself in the mirror.

Melanie spun her around once and slipped a pink cape over the front of Carina. "Relax, sweetie," she said in a soothing voice.

Carina took several deep breaths. She wasn't sure what sort of style Melanie had in store, but surely, a woman of her expertise would know what to do. Melanie dug into her thick, coily hair. Carina winced as Melanie tugged at the tangles with a comb. Her childhood tenderheadedness was still the bane of her existence.

"So, you've all known each other since college?" Carina asked, trying to take her mind off the pain.

"Pretty much," Delisa said, sorting through her vast makeup collection spread out at her station. "We're besties, sorority sisters, and used to be college roommates. The three of us were cosmetology majors, and Autumn was a photography major. After college, Autumn wanted to open a boudoir photography studio. This city had none, so she set up shop, and we all happily joined her. It was the best thing we'd ever done."

Emma rolled her eyes, fighting down a smile. "Speak for yourself, 'Li." She flicked her gaze to Carina. "I was roped into it."

Melanie chuckled, then said to Carina, "Emma is Autumn's little sister. All of us grew up in the same town in the mountains, so as far as I'm concerned, we're all clutchmates."

"Oh, for fuck's sake. Autumn's literally thirty seconds older than me because she hatched first," Emma retorted.

"She still has bragging rights, *chica,*" Delisa touted, wagging her finger.

Emma blew a raspberry.

Carina's gaze bounced between the three dragonesses, their lighthearted banter easing her tension. She admired the close camaraderie they had. It was something she'd hardly had in her life. People she thought she could trust ended up betraying her. She'd lost touch with the few college friends she had, after they had moved away. She'd grown accustomed to the single life, though she wasn't sure if she was truly happy.

Thirty minutes later, Carina's hair was combed out and washed. While Carina was under the dryer, Emma rolled a pedicure caddy and portable foot spa in front of her.

"I'll get your pedi done in a jiffy," Emma said. Then she prepared the water-filled foot spa.

Carina watched the water begin to bubble, and she smiled. Her body tingled in delight. In that moment, she really did feel like a queen. *What I wouldn't do to have a hot guy give me this kind of treatment.* As the fleeting thought crossed her mind, her smile disappeared. The thought of having a devoted man in her life was wishful thinking.

The hair dryer turned off just as Emma finished the pedicure. She put a pair of foam slippers onto Carina's feet, then Melanie ushered Carina back to the salon chair.

Carina watched as Melanie transformed her massive blow-out afro into a natural, curly twist-out style that complemented her soft, round face. When she finished, Melanie looked at Carina's reflection in the mirror. "*Voila.* The queen has arrived."

Carina did a double take, then blinked several times. She'd had many hairstyles, but none quite like this. Her jaw unhinged. She gently ran her fingers along the soft curls. "This... this looks amazing!" she said.

Melanie beamed. "Glad you like it. Now, all that's left is the mani and makeup, and then you'll be ready for your royal photoshoot." She swiped off the pink cape from around Carina and lowered the salon chair.

Carina's cheeks hurt from smiling so much. She stared down at her toes, which were covered in sparkling-green nail polish. *I can get used to this.*

For the remainder of the hour, Emma cleaned, refined, and polished her nails, and Delisa applied her exquisite artistic touches to her makeup. Once they were both done, Carina stared into the mirror a final time. Her eyes widened. Her reflection appeared nothing like herself. The person before her looked ten years younger with smooth russet skin that was flawless. Coupled with her trendy hairstyle, Carina wondered if she'd have a chance out in the world now. A chance to be noticed. A chance at love.

"I can't believe what I'm seeing right now," Carina said breathlessly.

Melanie, Emma, and Delisa gathered around her chair, all giggles and smiles.

"It's what we do," Melanie said, then extended her hand. "Come on. Time for your photoshoot."

Carina shrugged out of her robe and returned to the studio wearing her new lingerie. The room's cool temperature whisked over her exposed bare skin, inciting goosebumps. She spotted Autumn at one of the dressed-up sets busily moving a velvet-shaded lamp, and adjusting a chaise lounge.

Melanie cleared her throat. "Her Royal Highness is ready."

Autumn looked over her shoulder, her auburn hair whipping to the side. Her freckled face lit up like the sun. "Ohhh! She definitely is! Let the magical coronation begin!"

The next hour that went by seemed to drag on slower than mud. Carina was put through various poses in different intimate backdrops that were set up all around the studio. Some of the backdrops, like a bedroom scene, and even a dungeon scene, looked like something straight out of a cheesy X-rated flick. Carina still doubted that any of the photos would be worth salvaging by the time the shoot was done. She'd lost count on the number of reshoots and adjustments that Autumn had to do. Maybe Carina's figure wasn't photogenic enough. Maybe this whole boudoir thing wasn't for someone like her.

While Autumn was off developing the photos, Carina got dressed, and was escorted to a waiting area, a tiny room that sat between the lobby and main studio. Bright yellow-and-orange-beaded curtains covered the room's two doorways. The room contained a French-style wrought-iron two-seater bistro table that sat atop a white, fluffy shag rug. While she sat at the table and waited, Emma entered, carrying a silver platter of tea and sweet treats.

"Have some chai tea and homemade *alfajores*. Delisa baked them fresh this morning."

Carina eyed the delectable treats that looked like mini sandwich cookies topped with powdered sugar. She plucked one from the tray and took a small bite. "Mmm! Delicious."

Emma grinned. "Careful. They're addictive." She poured Carina a cup of tea and handed it to her. "Delisa loves making all sorts of Colombian sweets from her grandfather's home country."

"She's a great chef," Carina said, sipping the hot tea and shamelessly taking another *alfajor*.

Autumn rushed through the beaded curtain from the studio and waved a large manila envelope in the air. "All done!" the dragoness announced, a bright grin stretched over her freckled face.

"Ooh! I wanna see!" Emma said. She reached for the envelope, but Autumn held it away.

"Nope. It's for our dear queen's eyes only. Of course, if she wants to share them with you, then that is certainly her choice." Autumn handed the envelope to Carina. "Please look them over and make sure they are to your satisfaction. I don't accept payment from dissatisfied customers."

Carina took the envelope with two hands. It had some weight to it, and felt thick, like there was a book inside. She chewed her bottom lip. Her gaze shifted to Emma, whose curious eyes stared back at her with eager anticipation. Carina swallowed a tightness in her throat, and turned the envelope over. She slowly tugged on the security string and unwound it until the envelope's flap opened. Inside was a white photo album.

Carina widened her eyes. She carefully ran her hand over the album, which was embellished in gold trim. Gold calligraphic script etching the album's cover read: "A Queen's Coronation."

Smiling, she opened the album to the first page. Then she froze. She stared back at the image of herself in the green lingerie, posed atop the silk sheets of the bed prop from the bedroom backdrop. She wore an intense expression, fearless. *Did I really look like that?* she wondered. The photoshoot session was a blur, as her nerves and anxiety had swallowed her mind.

She flipped to the next page to another image of herself, this time, in the dungeon. The confident, daring expression that was on her face made her look like an entirely different woman. "This... can't be me... I don't look like this," she muttered.

"Oh, but it is!" Autumn insisted. "This is you. The *real* you! Embrace it."

"Are you sure you didn't just... manipulate this photo or something?"

Autumn's smile quickly faded, and her eyes flared with annoyance. "*Manipulate?* I think not! Everything you see in that album was from today's session. Do not doubt who you are, Carina. You are a queen, worthy to be revered as royalty."

Carina stared back at the photo, frowning.

Emma whipped her head back and forth. "Oooh, can't I just have a tiny peek, Autumn? *Pleeease?*" she begged.

"Are you satisfied with the photos or not?" Autumn asked, ignoring Emma.

Carina went through the rest of the pages in the album. They were all indeed beautiful, but she couldn't imagine that they were really her. That she was that photogenic as a thick girl in green lingerie. The men she'd met were all repulsed by that sort of thing. *Is the beautiful woman in this album really me?* "I... I like them..." she replied at last.

Autumn stared back at her for a moment, then nodded. "All right, then. You can pay Katie on your way out. It was a pleasure working with you. I do hope that one day you will embrace the beautiful queen that you truly are and take up your crown that is so rightfully yours. What I've told some of my past clients who were doubtful like you was to take that album everywhere you go. Carry it in your car, your purse... everywhere. That one moment you feel doubt, open the book, look at the photos and remind yourself of who you really are.

"You will soon get to a point where you won't need to carry the album around anymore. When that happens, then you would have ascended to royalty and become the woman you were meant to be."

Carina half-smiled, but it was short-lived. After returning to the lobby and paying for her session, she said goodbye to Autumn and the rest of the staff, then left. Back to the real world, and out of her royal fantasy.

CHAPTER 5

Diesel was lost in his own world of his favorite Viking death metal band, VanAesir, that thundered through his headphones, as he performed his last slow set of heavy squats. It was his downtime between clients. Carina wasn't on his schedule today, which meant the day dragged at tortoise speed.

He breathed out each count, sweat pouring down the sides of his face. He saw flashes of Carina in his mind and remembered a day he'd done weight training with her. Her thick thighs tightened and her big, gorgeous ass became perfectly round with each low squat. His tiger reeled in delight at the sight, yearning to come out and play. He wanted her, needed her, in every way possible. But he'd sensed her hesitation whenever she was around him. Doubt. The very thought of an insecure woman—a woman who was not happy with herself—was a complete turn-off for him. And yet, he couldn't stop thinking of the possibility of his tiger's intuition being wrong just once.

A notification sound dinged through his headphones, interrupting his musical trance. He completed his final repetition and reset the 260-pound-weighted bar back on its stand. Then he swiped up the towel from around his neck, dabbed sweat from his face and arms, and retrieved the phone from his bag, which sat on a bench beside him. What little excitement he had from thinking about Carina was quickly overtaken with dread, as Cammy's number flashed on the screen.

Fuck... Sighing, he answered the phone. "Hey."

"'Bout time you answered. What are you doing?" Cammy asked.

Diesel rolled his eyes. "I'm working. I have a job, unlike *some* people."

"I thought you owned that gym?"

"I do, but I still do personal training."

"Well, take a break, will you? I wanna see the sights of the city. One of my roommates said that I should check out a place called The Gyro's Journey. Do you know of it?"

"Eh, it's just some popular Mediterranean restaurant in town." *And one of Carina's favorite places*, he mused.

"Great! Let's go there today!"

Diesel blinked. "Today? As in right now?"

"Better now than never, Big Brother. Today is still my birthday."

He raked his fingers through his hair. He'd already called earlier that morning and gave her birthday wishes, and he'd hoped that she wouldn't ask for more. The last thing he needed was to go to a restaurant, run into Carina, and Cammy end up embarrassing him in front of her with her brashness. "Look, I'm busy here. I don't have time to go with you. Why don't you go with your roommates? Or take a cab there? Wouldn't that be a more fun way to spend your birthday than alone with me?"

There was a brief pause. "D, I came all this way to spend time with you. What's the harm in that?"

"That's bullshit, and you know it. You have an agenda. You're sticking your nose all up in my business and asking personal questions about my sex life. I don't need my little sister deciding when I find a mate."

"I'm not deciding. I'm just helping you along. Since you seem too scared to do it yourself. Who's that girl on your phone?"

He growled. "Bye, Cammy." He yanked the phone from his ear.

"No, don't hang up! Please, D!"

He paused, his thumb hovering over the End Call button as Cammy's pleading voice tugged at his heart. Letting out a deep sigh, he slowly brought the phone back to his ear.

"I'm sorry, D. I really am," she continued in a meek tone. "I just want to see you happy, that's all. Can we please have lunch together? Or an early dinner? At least do this for me just once for my birthday. I wanna hang out with you. I promise I won't ask you questions about that stuff anymore."

He shut his eyes a moment and rubbed his temple. She always knew what button to push to turn him into a teddy bear. And he knew there was no resisting her spell. "Fine," he said with another sigh.

"Yay! Thank you! Thank you! Come by here whenever you're done at work. Can't wait to hang out with you and stuff my face with gyros!" She ended the call.

Diesel stared at the lit-up screen sourly until it dimmed. A "date" with his little sister at a gyro bar—the cherry on top of his pathetic day.

CHAPTER 6

Carina sighed as the orange "service oil" light suddenly flashed on in the dashboard of her old, dark-blue hatchback. She chugged along with Main Street's Thursday traffic, the car's insistent sputtering a constant reminder of the numerous other problems she'd put off getting fixed. The car was the bane of her existence. Every time she got one thing fixed, something else broke. A vicious, money-sucking cycle. Oil changes were just about all the maintenance she'd kept up with on her car. As long as it got her where she needed to go, that was all that mattered.

With the rest of her day free, Carina drove to the nearest mechanic's shop for an oil change. She pulled up to the shop, which had opened just a few weeks ago and was conveniently located a few blocks away from the photo studio. It didn't look busy, much to her relief. She got out of her car and headed for the front office.

"Hello?" she called, realizing the office was empty. She suddenly heard the whirring of an air wrench coming from one of the adjacent garage bays. The noise stopped, and she called again, "Hello!"

Footsteps approached, and a man entered the office from a side door.

Carina's heart stopped for a moment as a pair of handsome dark-brown eyes stared back at her. There was something familiar about that gaze and the way it drove deep into her core. He was tall like Diesel, with a similar athletic physique. Spots of dirt and oil smeared the olive skin of his cheek, and along his tiger stripe-tattooed arms, but those imperfections added charm. The white oval-shaped name patch on the right breast of his navy-blue work shirt read "Gauge."

"Yes, miss. Can I help you?" he asked.

The sound of his low, enticing voice sent goosebumps down her arms. It reminded her of the way Diesel had captivated her when they'd first met. "H-Hi. I was wondering if you do walk-ins for oil changes?"

His lips formed a charming smile. "Yeah, sure. I can get you in and outta here quick."

"Thanks." She handed him her keys. As he took them from her, their hands touched briefly, long enough to send an electric sensation through every nerve in her body. Her breath hitched. *Damn. What was that?*

"Have a seat, and I'll be right back," he said, heading out the side door.

As soon as the door shut behind him, Carina exhaled a breath. Her nerves were still on edge, so she busied herself with checking for new messages on her phone. As usual, her prospects on the Plenti of Dates app were as dry as a bone. She sighed. *Am I just being too picky? Is it wrong for me to not want to date a guy who has no ambition and is still living with his mother?*

She closed the dating app, and her thoughts wandered back to Diesel. That was one man she was not picky about. He was everything she desired, but that was all he was—a helpless fantasy. He was her trainer and nothing more. Perhaps it was for the best that she didn't get too close to him in that way. But that didn't mean she had to stop seeing him, or training with him. He was helping her get into the best shape of her life in order for her to feel confident enough to finally find her one true love—wherever he was.

Maybe I can see him today, she thought. Now that her entire day was free, she had that luxury. But she'd never done walk-ins with him, and she had no idea what his schedule was like today. She dialed the number to Nine Stars Gym, but it was busy. Then she sent Diesel a text:

Carina: "can we trn 2day?"

She waited a few minutes, but there was no response. He was most likely busy with a client. She decided to stop by the gym after she left the auto shop.

Later, the side door opened, and Gauge returned with her keys. He stopped before her and smiled. She looked up at him, slightly openmouthed. The muscles in his tattooed forearms were bulging with small veins, a clear sign of his hard work. A small bead of sweat escaped his forehead and ran down the side of his face, getting lost under his shirt collar. Her mind wandered a moment, thinking about what he must look like under that shirt.

"All done, miss."

Snapping out of her thoughts, she stared at Gauge, who held her keys out to her. She hesitated then slowly took the keys, careful not to brush his hand again. "Thanks," she said then stood. "By the way, it's Carina."

His eyes narrowed with a look of interest. His smile grew. "Carina. Beautiful name for a beautiful woman."

She smiled, feeling her cheeks heat up. "Thank you." Already, he was working the charms. But her rational side nudged her, making her wonder if his flirting was for real or just another setup for pain. "So, what's the damage?" she asked, trying to steer the conversation away from herself.

Gauge looked her up and down. "For you, sweetie? Nothing."

She blinked. *Holy shit, is he serious?* "What? You can't possibly do a free oil change. Please let me know how much it is."

He laughed. "I own this shop, so I can do whatever I want."

She shook her head and fished through her purse for a ten-dollar bill. "Okay, then. How about a tip."

He gently pushed her hand away from him. "Don't worry about it."

Flustered, she bit her bottom lip. Even his strong yet gentle touch reminded her of Diesel. Damn, why did her personal trainer cloud her mind so much?

"Okay, tell you what. My assistant should be back from his lunch break anytime now. So how about you and I go get a bite to eat afterward?"

She lifted an eyebrow. *Did he just ask me out on a lunch date? A* lunch *date? This can't be real.* "I... I... uh..." Before she could finish her reply, the office's front door opened, and another man entered, dressed similarly to Gauge, but his physique was more like a bear's—tall and husky. His oval name patch read "Barron." He casually sucked on the straw of a cup from one of the nearby fast-food places. He eyed Carina and gave her a little wave before giving Gauge a pointed look and heading toward the side door leading to the work area.

Gauge watched him leave then rolled his eyes and shook his head with a smile. "Perfect timing.

That's Barron, my assistant and a good friend. He doesn't say much, but he's a damn good worker."

"Is he your only employee?" Carina asked.

Gauge nodded. "For now. I've only been open for two weeks. Work is slow, but steady, and Barron and I can handle things for now."

"That's good to hear. Your shop is in a good location."

"Thanks." He paused and looked at her expectantly. "So? You joining me for lunch or what?"

She was about to agree, when she glanced at the time on her phone. It was nearing four o'clock. Maybe Diesel would be able to see her if he wasn't too busy. She sighed and acknowledged Gauge with an apologetic look. "Damn. I'm sorry. Can I take a rain check? I want to see if my personal trainer can squeeze me in for a training session at the gym."

He shrugged and nodded. "Yeah, sure. Which gym?"

"Nine Stars. Over on the other side of town."

He looked thoughtful for a moment, then a slight pinch appeared on his brow. "Can't say that I've heard of that place. I'm new in town, only been living here for a little over a month." He shrugged it off. "Oh well. Do what you gotta do, I guess."

Carina noted the disappointed tone in his voice. She couldn't believe she'd just refused a date from such a hot guy. *What the hell is wrong with me?* She was usually the one on the receiving end of rejection, but she didn't like being on *either* end. Gauge seemed genuine in wanting to hang out. Since he worked at a grungy place, maybe he didn't prefer his women to be perfect, stick-thin pinup girls. Carina was certainly interested in knowing more about him.

"Why don't we do something this weekend?" she offered.

His face brightened slightly. "I'd like that."

"Okay." She took out her phone. "Let's exchange numbers."

He pulled out his phone from his back pocket. After they exchanged numbers, Carina checked her messages to see if Diesel had responded, but he still hadn't. She tucked her phone back in her purse and acknowledged Gauge. "All right. I'll see you this weekend, then?"

His charming smile returned. "It's a date, Ms. Carina."

A date. Carina fidgeted with her hands and chewed her bottom lip as she looked at him. Even his smile carried a striking resemblance that played with her thoughts.

CHAPTER 7

DIESEL LEANED HIS ELBOW ON the table, resting his cheek in his palm as he stared across the table at Cammy, who pigged out on a super-sized mutton gyro oozing with tzatziki sauce. The Gyro's Journey was packed as usual, but they were able to score a table—the very last vacant one—in the back corner of the restaurant.

"Mmm! No wonder this is such a popular place!" Cammy gushed. She took another hefty bite of the pita-wrapped delicacy. Her cheeks bulged as she chewed, a dollop of white tzatziki pasted on one corner of her mouth.

Spending time here with Cammy had sapped Diesel's appetite. This was Carina's favorite restaurant, and part of him wished it were her sitting across the table instead of his little sister.

"Whaff wron? Not eating?" Cammy asked with her mouth full.

"I'm not hungry." Diesel pulled out his phone and checked his messages. His last client for the day had been a no-show, which allowed him to get off work earlier than usual. Still, he'd checked his phone periodically to make sure his employees, or one of his clients weren't trying to contact him. His attention drew an unread message from Carina that was sent two hours ago. His heart fluttered, then sank. He'd been so caught up with trying to keep Cammy happy, he'd completely missed the message. Just when he thought this day couldn't get any worse. He couldn't wait to go home at last and finally forget about this day ever happening at all.

"Why're you so grumpy?" Cammy said, and he snapped out of his thoughts. "Aren't you even happy to spend time with me?"

No. Yes. Fuck... He rubbed his hand over his face and let out an exasperated sigh. "You didn't exactly come visit at the most convenient time for me."

Cammy regarded him dubiously, then picked up her bottle of beer—Deerhopper brand triple IPA, her favorite independent label. "Oh yeah? And tell me, what time would have been 'most convenient' for you? You're a mess, Big Brother. I would've expected that from the rest of the family, but not you."

He flicked his gaze at her as she guzzled the dark liquid, and pursed his lips. She'd been right about that; he really didn't give a shit about clan politics, after he'd lost his shot at the throne. But the idea of becoming a leader—an alpha—had still continuously crossed his mind. "I'm nothing like those sons of bitches," Diesel said at last. "Don't ever compare me to them."

"It's just an observation." Cammy took another big bite out of her gyro.

He shut off his phone and stuffed it in his pocket. "I left to find my own way..." He pinned her with a stern gaze. "Find my *own* mate."

She stared back at him, unfazed. "I swear, D. For someone bent on doing things your own way, you sure make no damn sense at all. You've obviously found your mate already, but you're too chickenshit to do anything about it. What's up with that?"

He gritted his teeth. It was bad enough he was rejected by his own family after his losing in battle. He was very afraid—afraid of being rejected yet again by the woman he craved.

"Axle is hardly alpha material," Cammy continued. "He demands respect, but everyone shits all over him. There is no more order in the clan.

"But the way you're acting right now, like you seem to have no idea how to claim a mate, that is not an alpha, either. At least Axle has more balls than you in that regard."

Diesel sneered. "I *am* an alpha."

"I know fear when I smell it, Big Brother, and frankly, you stink. If Aunt Evaline were here, she would tear everybody's asses apart for allowing the clan to spiral this badly."

The mention of his late aunt raised a shiver up his spine. As mean as she was, she was also the most respected and feared alpha of the Whitetide Streak. It seemed that Axle still could not fill her big shoes, even after claiming victory over his battle with Diesel.

He stared at Cammy long and hard for a moment. His mind, still flooded with thoughts of his aunt Evaline, started playing with his vision.

Soon, Cammy's face began to shift into his aunt's image, as though her ghost had possessed his sister. Then the world around him shifted to a time and place of long ago, in the backyard training grounds with his cub-siblings and Aunt Evaline.

"Stop fucking around, cub," his aunt had told them when they were younger. However, she kept a stern eye on Diesel as she spoke, as though everything was directed to him. *"You have the blood of royalty—tiger's blood. You are clan Whitetide."*

"Yes, ma'am," Diesel's younger self had said, a practiced reply to his former matriarch.

"This clan was not built on weakness, but the blood and determination of the strong," Evaline continued. *"When the time comes, it will be time for you all to find mates. You must remain fearless in your search for your life-bond. Fear is what's going to tear this clan apart."*

"D? Are you listening to me?"

Diesel started, rubbed his eyes, and his aunt's image was gone. He blinked several times, as if awakening from a dream, then stared back at Cammy's pouty face. "Yeah, sure," he said absently.

She scowled. "Man, you're totally wrecked. Maybe I *should* get that train ticket and go someplace else."

He perked up a little as he struggled to make sense of his flustered mind. His aunt's words. *Fear is what's tearing this clan apart...*

"Carina... Her name is Carina," he blurted.

Cammy scrunched her brow. "Huh?"

"The girl on my phone," he continued. Then he pinned her a dubious look. "Since you wanted to know so bad."

"Hey, I promised before I wouldn't ask about it, so..."

"I know you want to know who she is. I call her Ri for short. She's beautiful, though she's self-conscious about things like her weight and body shape, but I find them perfect on her. She's had one too many bad relationships in the past and is convinced that all men hate women with extra weight."

Cammy frowned a little. "That's a shame. Not the first time I've heard that story, though, unfortunately."

Diesel let his mind wander a moment, and then he sighed. "She inspires me. She's like a breath of fresh air. I always look forward to every day I get to train her. She's the reason why I love my job."

"She sounds like a cool girl."

"She is. As her personal trainer, I'm helping her get to her goal weight and size. But I think it's a waste of time. I hope she never reaches it. I love her the way she is right now. She's trying so hard to impress these asshole guys.

"She sees me as her personal trainer and nothing more. A professional student-teacher relationship, y'know? I don't think the possibility of us together has ever crossed her mind."

"Do you know that for sure?" Cammy asked with raised eyebrows.

Diesel shrugged. "No, but as you've seen, I always get the shitty end of the stick in life, so I can only assume this is another instance. I'm tired of it all. I've lost just about everything around me. I don't want to jeopardize losing Carina, too, if I make advances and she's not even interested."

"I think she just needs a little nudge in your direction. Even if it's just enough to think about the possibilities."

He shook his head. "No... it's... not right. She's my student."

"And?"

He blinked at her. "'And'? It's a conflict of interest. I have to stay away. For my sanity's sake. I'm into her, but I don't want to ruin a good thing. If I wasn't her trainer, things would have been much different."

"Fuck that. Fuck morals. Fuck the rules. Go claim her, damn it." She wolfed down the rest of her gyro and finished her beer.

One corner of his lips tugged upward into a small smile. Cammy told it like it was, and he wasn't upset about it. If only he had that same carefree spirit, but his stubbornness always seemed to best his willpower.

She glanced toward the line of people at the front counter and rubbed her chin pensively. "Hmm... I think I'll get another gyro. That one was soooo good."

Diesel gawked at her. "Are you fucking serious? That thing was huge! How can you *still* be hungry after all that?" *And where in the hell does she put all that food?*

"Don't judge me. I'm listening to my body. Isn't that what you always tell your clients?" She paused, brought her fist to her lips, and belched loudly. "Whoa! 'Scuse me... Sounds like my body's telling me it wants another gyro. And maybe I'll try out those chicken kabobs, too." She scooted out of the booth and skipped happily toward the front counter.

Speechless, Diesel continued staring at her. Then a familiar figure appeared in his periphery from the front entrance. A plus-sized curvy woman walked in, wearing a frumpy, oversized T-shirt, and a pair of dark-green leggings. But her thick, curly hair was done up in a beautiful twist-out style, and her makeup was on point, like she'd just stepped out of the beauty salon. She scanned the restaurant, a bewildered expression etched on her flawless, light-brown face.

He did a double take, and his heart fluttered faster than a hummingbird.

It was Carina.

CHAPTER 8

Carina's entire world stopped as she found herself staring eye to eye with Diesel, who was sitting alone at the back of the restaurant. To her surprise and delight, her suspicions were correct in that it was his car she'd seen parked out front while she was on her way home from her brief visit at the gym.

She smiled at him from afar and gave him a small wave. A few seconds later, he waved back. He didn't take his eyes off her. She glanced around the restaurant, wondering if he was alone. Sure seemed like it. The line to the front counter was almost out the door, so Carina wandered over to Diesel's table.

"Hi, D," she greeted.

His smile faltered, and a look of guilt beset his eyes. "Hey. Sorry I missed your text. I totally got sidetracked."

"It's okay. It was sort of an impromptu thing, so I didn't think you'd have time to see me anyway."

He shook his head. "Trust me, if I would've checked my phone earlier, I would've definitely wanted to see you. I was actually surprised to see your text today, since this is normally your workday."

"Yeah, my boss called me off today. For the first time in the two years I started working there. It can't be a good sign…"

"Damn, I'm sorry."

"It's okay. I made myself busy today." She left it at that, hoping Diesel wouldn't prod further.

"Well, it's good to see you again," he said. Then his gaze cut to something behind her, and his face paled. "Ah…"

"Hmm?" Carina looked over her shoulder. A young, orange-brown-haired woman wearing a white crop top, black shorts, purple fishnet stockings, and black studded, calf-high combat boots walked in her direction from the front counter, carrying a tray with a giant gyro, chicken kabobs, and a bottle of beer. She hummed a lighthearted tune as she drew nearer. She and Carina locked eyes.

The other woman stopped humming and smiled. "Hello!" she greeted cheerily. Then she brushed past Carina and took a seat at the table with Diesel.

Carina chewed her bottom lip. The woman was gorgeous—fit, thin, and the perfect type for guys like Diesel. Carina should've known that Diesel wouldn't be eating alone. She suddenly felt two inches tall. "Ah... I... I'm sorry, I didn't realize—"

Diesel perked up. "Whoa! No... *Hell no,* it's not what you think. This is Cammy Reed, my sister."

Carina suddenly felt a great weight lift from her chest. *Sister?*

Cammy took a bite of her gyro, then studied Carina as she chewed. As she swallowed, her face lit up. "Oh! Are you Carina? You look totally different from D's picture."

"Yes, I'm Carina... what picture?" She swiveled her gaze to Diesel. *He has pictures of me?* Her heart deflated a little. *Has he been showing them to people? Making fun of me? Is he just another dirtbag?*

"She mistook you for a picture of one of the trainers at the gym," Diesel said quickly, then shot Cammy a glare. "Didn't you?"

Cammy rolled her eyes and shrugged. "Whatever."

Carina's throat tightened at the thought of such a betrayal. The one guy she'd trusted to help her be happier and more accepting of herself would end up being the biggest piece of shit she'd ever met.

She looked back toward the front counter and noticed the line had barely moved. Suddenly, she no longer craved Greek food. She just wanted to go home, curl up in her bed, and forget today ever happened.

"I need to go. See you later, D. Nice meeting you, Cammy," Carina said in a slightly choked-up voice.

Diesel opened his mouth, as though he were about to reply, then closed it.

Cammy narrowed her eyes at Carina, then pointed. "Hold on. That awesome eyeliner is starting to run. Might want to make a quick detour to the ladies' room before you go."

"What?" As if something else could go wrong. Carina's queenly makeup job was already fading away, it seemed. She gently patted her cheeks, then looked at her fingers, which were clean. "Are you sure it's running?"

"Mmhmm." Cammy swallowed another greedy bite of her gyro then stood. "I'll help you out. Follow me." She strode past Carina down a short hallway at the back of the restaurant where the bathrooms were.

Carina looked from Cammy back to Diesel, who had his elbow leaned on the table and his face buried in his palm. Carina pursed her lips. *He's not even looking at me anymore. Is he embarrassed about me? Because of my makeup? Or does he not want to be seen with me in a public place, outside of his gym?* Her mind swam with so many thoughts and scenarios, and it further stung her aching heart.

She finally trudged after Cammy and went through the door of the ladies' room. They were alone in the small, two-stalled bathroom. Cammy leaned against the sink with her arms crossed and regarded Carina with an amused smirk.

"Sorry, I lied," Cammy said. "Your makeup's not running. But I still want to talk to you."

Carina arched an eyebrow. "About what?"

"About my brother."

Carina's throat tightened. Small beads of sweat formed on her palms. "What about him? And what was that about pictures of me? Has he been secretly sharing pictures of me to strangers?"

"What? No. He would never do that. I know that for a fact. He's told me some stuff about you, though."

There it was. She hardened her gaze. "What sort of 'stuff'?"

"Good stuff," Cammy assured. "He's been gushing about you ever since I arrived yesterday. He said you're in inspiration."

Carina's heart jumped a little. "Me? An inspiration? Surely, not to him. In case you hadn't noticed, I'm nowhere near his caliber of fitness."

Cammy shrugged. "Hey, I'm just telling you what he said. He's always excited on the days that he gets to train you. You're the reason why he loves his job."

Carina blinked several times. "Are you sure we're talking about the same Diesel Reed?"

Cammy laughed. "Yes. Don't tell him I told you that, though. He gets all grumpy with a stick up his ass when I talk about his feelings to other people—especially to people he likes."

Carina swiveled her gaze from Cammy and stared at the mirror, a bit taken aback. All of this information was coming faster than she could process it. *Did he really say that about me?* she wondered. *Is he really into me like that?*

Cammy's reflection sidled beside her, and she stared back at Carina with an amused grin. "Did I mention I *really* like your makeup? It looks so professionally done."

"Thanks," she said absently, trying to gather her thoughts. "Sorry, I… I didn't know Diesel had a sibling."

"He never told you?" Cammy blew a raspberry. "Figures… Well, there are four of us blood siblings, actually. But we don't talk about the other two."

"Two more sisters?"

"No, brothers."

Carina nodded. *Two brothers… are they both like Diesel? Will I ever meet them sometime?*

"Anyway," Cammy continued. "I was wondering if, since you're a friend of Diesel's, we can hang out sometime and you can show me around the city. This is my first time in New Rochford. Diesel's too embarrassed to hang out with his little sister, and he acts all weird whenever I ask if he can take me sightseeing."

Carina smiled slightly. "Sure. What are some things you like to do?"

"Mmm..." Cammy tapped her chin. "I like museums, nature trails, shopping, food trucks, arcades..."

"Well, there's plenty of that and more here."

"Actually, what's the fanciest restaurant in this city?"

Carina blinked. "Fancy?"

"Yeah. As in pinky-finger-out-fancy-schmansy."

"Uh... that would be Blue Iris Fusion. But people only go there for special occasions."

Cammy clapped her hands together. "Great. Why don't you and I go there this Friday?"

Carina blinked. "Uh, didn't you hear me? People only go there for special occasions."

"Yeah, I heard you. This is my first time seeing Diesel in literally years. It's a big deal for me, so yeah, I would consider this an extra special occasion. Will you join me? It'll be my treat."

"Well..."

"I should drag Diesel along, too, actually. This is not only my birthday week, but also a reunion celebration, so naturally, he should be there."

Carina opened her mouth to reply, then closed it. The thought of the three of them at a fancy restaurant together made her heart race with anxiety. "Um… maybe you two should—"

"No, I want you there, too. Besides, I'm sure Diesel won't be in much of a talking mood, so you and I can talk. Still, I like the idea of my brother being there while we celebrate together. Pleeease will you join us?" Cammy clasped her fingers together, giving her a wide, puppy-dog-eye stare.

Carina chewed her bottom lip, the pleading tone in Cammy's voice tugging at her heart. Part of her wanted to see Diesel again, but she'd wondered if their little Friday outing would turn him off in the end. As much as she'd crushed over him, she was also careful to not overstep her bounds and destroy the teacher/student relationship they had going at the gym. But Cammy seemed like she knew just how to handle her brother. "O… Okay," she said at last.

Cammy beamed. "Excellent! I'll take care of everything. Just don't tell Diesel, will you? He's going to get grumpy again if he finds out I'm dragging him out."

"I won't tell him," Carina said, smiling slightly.

"Great! I'll see you Friday, then."

After they exchanged numbers, Cammy walked out of the bathroom, leaving Carina alone with her thoughts. She stared back at her reflection in the mirror and sighed, a small smile hinting at her face. She'd only just met Cammy, and she already liked her fun and outgoing personality. Men probably liked her, too. She had the looks on top of all that. She had the whole package that guys tended to dig. Maybe if Carina hung around her a bit more, she might get lucky and work a miracle on her relationship status.

Maybe…

CHAPTER 9

THIRTEEN... FOURTEEN... FIFTEEN... DIESEL exhaled a deep sigh as he released the four-hundred-pound weights of the leg press machine. He relished the burning sensation in his calves and thighs, which kept him from letting his mind wander too much about yesterday's restaurant outing with Cammy. It was all he could do after the disaster she'd caused.

And to do it right in front of Carina.

Diesel let out a low growl of frustration. He had no idea what Cammy and Carina had talked about in the bathroom. He sensed it wasn't anything good when he saw Carina walk out of the bathroom and head straight for the exit, not even stopping to say goodbye.

Cammy had only been here for two days, and she had already begun to ruin his life.

This is what I get for being nice.

He set his feet on the floor and gave his legs a good, long stretch. His ten a.m. appointment would soon arrive, and to his disappointment, it wasn't going to be Carina. She wasn't on his schedule today, which meant it was going to be another shitty day. This time, however, he frequently checked his phone for new messages, in case Carina asked for another impromptu training session. Even though he didn't want to miss her this time, he wondered if she would ever message him like that again after what happened yesterday.

As Diesel guzzled water from his bottle, his phone chirped with a ringtone that indicated his sister was calling. Groaning, he swiped it up and checked the screen. He'd half a mind to reject the call, but that would probably mean she'd come down to his gym and embarrass him in front of his peers. Grinding his teeth, he reluctantly answered the call. "What do you want?"

"Geez. How big is that stick up your ass today?" Cammy said.

He growled. "Look, I'm busy. I got a client coming in soon, so unless it's important..."

"I'll make it quick. I was wondering if we can go to Blue Iris Fusion tomorrow night."

He blinked several times. "Blue Iris Fusion? That expensive-ass restaurant?"

"Yeah. My roomie said it's one of the fanciest in town. I wanna go check it out. I'll buy. I've got enough splurging money saved up."

"People don't just go there on a whim. It's a special place. You gotta dress up and shit."

"Well, *duh*. Of course you gotta dress up. I just want to go there for the experience. Since, y'know, they don't have fancy restaurants in Whitetide Falls. Can you believe I've never been to one before? What better time than now, when I can experience it with my favorite big brother?"

Diesel wrinkled his nose. "That's bullshit. The way you travel all over the place, how have you not been to a fancy restaurant?"

"It's true. I've never been to one. But only because I've never been to a place that had one. Now's my chance, and I want to take it. So will you go with me? Please?"

"No," he snapped. "Go with your roommate. I'm done with you. You've embarrassed me for the last time."

"How did *I* embarrass *you?*"

Diesel paused a beat. "What did you two talk about in the bathroom, huh?"

"Nothing. I was helping Carina with her makeup."

"Bullshit! Her makeup was fine. What the fuck did you tell her? Were you talking about me?"

"For fuck's sake, Diesel! What's with all the paranoia? Why does it matter to you what Carina and I talk about?"

"Because, I don't want you spreading lies about me."

"When have I ever done that?"

He opened his mouth, ready to reply, then paused and thought about the question. She'd never explicitly spread lies, but she had her way of twisting truths.

"Look," Cammy continued. "I'm not in the business of ruining whatever you and Carina got going on."

"There's nothing going on."

"Now *that's* bullshit. Honestly. I think it's cute you have a crush on her."

"I don't have a 'crush'… Fucking hell, just drop it already."

"Fine. So can we have dinner together at Blue Iris Fusion, then? Pleeease?"

Exasperated, Diesel closed his eyes and rubbed his temple. That tone in her voice again always snagged him like a fish to bait. "All right. Here's the deal. This is the absolute *last time* we're going to do this 'hanging out' shit. The last. Time. Understand?"

An audible sigh of relief came through the speaker. "Yes! Yes! I understand. I promise. This is the last time."

"And for fuck's sake, do *not* embarrass me."

"I won't, I promise. I'll make sure Friday night is a positive night. I'll pay for all the food and everything, so you don't have to worry. It's all on me."

He rolled his eyes. "Yeah. Whatever… What time do you want to go?"

"Hmmm… I'll try and get a reservation for seven o'clock. Cool?"

He briefly thought about his schedule for tomorrow. Fridays were usually his lighter days, and Carina was also on his schedule in the afternoon, which made it even more exciting. "Seven works," he said.

"Awesome! Thanks. I love you, Big Brother. See you tomorrow."

The back of his throat tightened. She'd rarely showed such affection unless she really meant it, and even then, she'd only showed that affection toward him. Unlike the rest of his family, he was always there for her, like a security blanket. He couldn't help but smile, as he felt his heart tugging in all directions. "Love you, too. Now leave me alone."

CHAPTER 10

FRIDAY. NORMALLY, DIESEL WOULD BE excited, but dread had haunted him the entire day, even during his session with Carina. Seven o'clock was approaching fast. Diesel could barely concentrate on Carina's training as he thought about what crazy mess Cammy would pull him into at Blue Iris Fusion. Even though she'd promised to behave, she was still as mischievous as a cub, and he'd learned to take her promises with a grain of salt.

Still, he loved his sister, and wanted the best for her, even if she did drive him bonkers sometimes. As much as he hated her clinging to him all the time, he understood the need to be there for her.

To turn his back on her would make him like the rest of his family he'd swore he'd never become.

Bam! Bam! Bam!

Diesel snapped out of his thoughts as Carina kicked and punched the focus pads in a rhythmic set of cardio drills and patterns during the final minutes of the training session. Smiling, he watched her, his eyes following the way her body jiggled and moved with every hit. He'd imagined what that beautiful body would look like cinched in a dress that defined every curve. His tiger approved. He clenched his jaw. *No, I gotta get over her, dammit.*

As he mentally wrestled with himself, trying to stave off his desire for her, he also heard his sister's voice echo in his mind.

"...Fuck morals. Fuck the rules. Go claim her, damn it..."

Carina's face seemed distant, however, as if she had something on her mind. It fed into his feline curiosity.

After Carina finished her last drill, Diesel called it a day. She took a seat on the bench and dabbed her face with a small hand towel.

"Everything okay?" Diesel asked, deciding to sate that curiosity.

She rubbed the towel down her neck. His eyes followed, lingering there a moment then drawing down to the glistening skin of her chest. Her nipples were so erect and prominent beneath the tank top that he desperately wanted to pinch and flick the distinct little pebbles with his thumbs. Her breasts were the perfect size: full, round, and large enough to palm in his hands. It took all his willpower to keep from pinning her to the floor, ripping off that top, and sucking greedily on them, tugging those rock-hard nipples with his teeth.

He mentally swore at the fantasy.

"I'm fine," she said, her voice making him haul his gaze back to her face.

The fantasy still lingered in his mind, and his hard dick strained in his shorts. He cleared his throat, trying to mentally work down his arousal. "Got any plans this weekend?"

She guzzled water from her bottle then smiled slightly. "Not really. Maybe I'll go clubbing or something."

"Alone?"

"Yeah, probably. Maybe I'll meet someone at the club. That'll be something, huh?" She gave a hollow laugh.

Staring at her, he swallowed a lump in his throat. The fact that she was actively going out meeting people made his heart sink. It wouldn't be long until someone came along and snagged her. And she would be gone forever. His tiger didn't approve. But he couldn't claim a mate who didn't desire him. "Sounds exciting," he said in an absent tone.

She laughed again. "I wouldn't call it exciting. Though, I guess it might be the apocalypse or something if I end up running into a guy who's interested in me. I'll finally see if all this training was worth it."

"I'm sure whatever guy you meet will appreciate someone like you," he said, his voice slightly choked as he tried to sound supportive. "And hell yeah, all your training will be worth it, because I trained you."

Her smile faltered slightly. "Yeah, you did..."

The wistful tone of her voice didn't go unnoticed. "You sure you're okay?"

She nodded quickly and began packing her things into her duffel bag. "I'm fine. Just... a little nervous about what the weekend will bring."

"It can be scary, going out and meeting people," he said. The fear and doubt emanating from her made him wonder if she was already having second thoughts about her weekend plans.

"Thanks for the workout, D. I'll see you later." With her duffel bag slung over her shoulder, she headed for the showers.

At six thirty, Diesel hopped into his newly detailed black convertible. As soon as he started the engine, his phone rang. Cammy's name flashed on the screen. A bitter taste formed in his mouth. "Yeah?" he answered.

"Hey, Bro. Um... I'm not ready yet, so can you just meet me there instead of picking me up?" Cammy said meekly.

Diesel blinked. "Are you fucking serious?"

"I'm very serious! I went shopping, and it took me forever to find the perfect outfit to wear tonight. Then I washed my hair, and it's taking forever to dry."

He gritted his teeth. "Cam, I swear, if you're setting me up, I'm going to kick your ass. Making me go through all this trouble to wear this fucking suit and shit..."

"No. Please, just go ahead and meet me at the restaurant. I'll take a taxi and head down there when I'm done."

He scowled. *Glad this is the last damn time I'll be doing this shit...* "Hurry up!" he barked, then ended the call before she had a chance to reply. He tore out of his driveway and floored the accelerator.

By six fifty, Diesel arrived in front of the elusive Blue Iris Fusion which sat on Grandway Square Boulevard in the heart of downtown New Rochford. He glanced at the cars that were parallel parked along the curb and found a parking space of his own. After getting situated, Diesel got out of the car and checked his reflection in one of its side windows. He adjusted his tie and smoothed out the creases in his dark-grey suit jacket. He couldn't remember the last time he'd gotten this dressed up before, and was surprised the suit still fit. Finally, he ran his fingers through his hair, removing last-minute tangles. Afterward, he headed for the restaurant's entrance, where a dark-haired waiter in a tuxedo stood behind a white podium with gold trim. He flicked his gaze at Diesel, his blue eyes briefly giving off a faint golden glow in the light. Diesel straightened, sensing the wolf in him.

"Yes, sir, may I help you?" the man asked, his tone a mix of reservation and annoyance.

Diesel marched up to the podium. "Yeah, my sister made a reservation here for seven o'clock. Under the name Cammy Reed."

The waiter scanned a small tablet computer and nodded curtly. "Ah, yes. Right this way, sir."

As Diesel entered the restaurant, its soft blue-tinted interior was welcoming. The waiter ushered him through the sea of tables, which were mostly occupied by couples. Various types of shifters shrouded in their human forms piqued Diesel's senses, reminding him to keep his own inner beast in check. The waiter directed Diesel to a table by a window and set down a single-sided leather-bound menu. Diesel seated himself while he gave the area another once-over.

His mind raced. Being in this place surrounded by so many couples unnerved him. The restaurant reeked with love, something he still didn't have. Why Cammy decided to come to this place was beyond him.

He whipped out his phone from his suit jacket's inner pocket and sent a text to Cammy.

D: i'm here.

Moments later, Cammy responded.

Cam: Cool! :)

He blinked. *What the hell does* that *even mean?* The more he wondered, the more he felt like a complete ass. *Did she really stand me up?* He scowled. *Fuck being nice. I'm gonna—*

"D..."

He sniffed once and froze. *Oh shit...* He looked toward the source of the surprised female voice.

The last woman he'd expected to see.

CHAPTER 11

Carina... Diesel widened his eyes. She was dressed in an elegant plum off-the-shoulder dress that cinched every inch of her curves. The neckline plunged just enough to reveal her bountiful cleavage. Her hair was styled in a wild, coily afro, perfectly complementing her gently made-up face. Light powder grazed her caramel-toned cheeks, accenting her high cheekbones and big brown eyes.

His heart swelled. Relief spread through his body like a wave, but the sensation quickly turned to pain once it reached his dick. Carina was deliciously sexy, and his tiger was ready to pounce and claim her. He scrambled out of his chair. "C-

Carina! W-What are you doing here?" he asked, his voice cracking.

She smiled softly. "I was here to help celebrate."

He furrowed his brow. "Celebrate what?"

"You and Cammy. It's been a while since you two have seen each other, right? So weren't we celebrating your reunion?"

Reunion? His jaw dropped. Then he swiveled his gaze to the table, which was only set for two. His mind finally put the puzzle together. *Oh, for fuck's sake...* "Did Cammy put you up to this?"

Carina cocked her head. "What do you mean? She invited me, so..."

He slapped his forehead. *Dammit, Cam!* "I'm sorry. It was all bullshit. Look, let's get out of here. I'll explain later."

Another tuxedo-clad waiter approached their table. He adjusted his thin, round glasses, and offered Diesel and Carina a curious glance. "Pardon me. Is everything all right? Are the accommodations not to your satisfaction?"

Diesel cleared his throat, sensing the owl shifter beneath the stoic man's guise. "Everything's fine. We've come here by mistake. Apparently, my sister played a prank. Sorry for wasting your time. I really can't afford this place, so I think it's best we leave."

The waiter scrunched his brow. "Afford? Wait, sir. There is a five-hundred-dollar credit applied to your RSVP. You do not owe anything at this time."

Diesel blinked. *Five hundred dollars?* Then he remembered his chat with Cammy the day before. *She was handling everything. She had this planned all along.* He looked at Carina. "Actually, let's stay."

She gave him a slow, curious nod. "O... kay?"

"We'll stay," he confirmed with the waiter, and then the man left. Diesel pulled out the opposite chair for Carina, then patted its cushioned backrest. "Sit."

After some hesitation, she lowered herself in the seat. "Well, that was... strange."

Diesel returned to his chair across from her. "It's all Cammy's doing. I should've known she'd be up to something."

Carina smiled reassuringly. "It's okay. I like Cammy. She seems like a fun person to be around. Did she really set all this up for... *us*?" She met Diesel's gaze.

Us... His tiger lingered on her stare for several moments. She didn't seem to mind Cammy's little prank, and he sensed a hint of relief in her voice. *Is Carina glad this happened?* A small chill ran through his body. "Yeah, it seems that way," he said at last.

"Well, we might as well make the most of it, especially if it's your sister's treat. That was really nice of her, considering she recently had a birthday.

"It was yesterday. She turned twenty-four." His heart pounded, a burning question on the tip of his tongue. His feline curiosity had to know. "So, I guess this is a date then," he said with a half-hearted chuckle.

Carina started, a hint of pink hinting her cheeks. "D-Date? What makes you think that?"

He blinked at her reaction. *Maybe she doesn't want this.* "Well, I just thought, since it's the two of us at a place like this, and..." He blew out a puff of air. "Never mind..."

"We're just hanging out, D. I mean, we know each other already. And you're my trainer."

He clenched his jaw. She'd given excuses, but she didn't exactly say 'no,' either. *Fuck morals. Fuck the rules.* He'd restrained his tiger's desires for so long, he couldn't think straight. Now, he mustered the courage to allow his inner beast to finally take control. "And?" he challenged.

Her forehead knotted in confusion. Then she leaned her head closer to him and said in a low voice, "And? I can't date my personal trainer."

"Why not?"

"Because it's... you know... weird? Conflict of interest and all that?"

"So?"

She rolled her eyes then put both hands on the table in frustration. "Don't you have rules against dating your clients?"

"Fuck the rules."

She stared at him blankly. "So you're telling me you've dated your previous clients before?"

"No."

She gave him a dubious look then let out a small laugh. "You're lying."

"Why would I lie about that?" He noticed a waitress approaching their table and waved her off. Her timing couldn't have been any worse. Carina was on the defense and could easily walk out at any time if he didn't handle things right. He reached across the table for her hand and stared carefully into her eyes. "You honestly think I've dated my past clients?"

Pursing her lips, she yanked her hand away then exhaled through her nose. "Don't kid yourself. I know you have. And you know what? That's your business. But *this*..." She made a hand gesture between them, "...can't be a date. Not me and you."

"Why not?"

"Because I'm not supposed to be with a guy like you."

He arched an eyebrow. "A guy like me?"

"You're a fucking athlete, D. Ripped as hell. You can have any woman you want. Me being a thick girl is a huge contrast with what you do for a living. We just don't look right together."

He gritted his teeth, controlling the deep growl that rumbled in his throat. He stared at her with a gaze so intense that the colors in his vision slowly lost their saturation. His tiger was yearning to break free, to hunt and kill every man who dared hurt her, but he continued to fight it back.

"Listen," he snapped in a low tone. "I told you before not to lump me with the rest of your previous fucktard boyfriends. I don't know what you think I am, but I am no monster to mistreat a woman because of her looks. That's just fucking stupid. And I don't give two shits about what we look like together. And for your information, I happen to love thick women—very much like you."

She stared at him, slightly openmouthed and speechless.

He continued in a calmer tone, "You wanna know the truth? I like you, 'Ri. Ever since you walked through the front doors of my gym and requested me to be your personal trainer."

Her cheeks reddened, and she averted her gaze to the white tablecloth, where she drew small circles with her finger. "I... I don't know what to say."

His smile returned. "Don't say anything. Let's order some food." He beckoned one of the nearby waitresses.

After they ordered, Carina eventually found her voice, and the more she talked, the more Diesel sensed her denial. She went on about their gym schedules and dating, and how they lived opposite lifestyles, but he only half listened. She had the wrong idea about him, and he intended to change that. His tiger's confidence grew the more he listened to her. Beneath her doubts and fears, he sensed a strong woman, and that was what truly attracted his tiger. Even after their food arrived, he could barely concentrate on his steak dinner as he thought about how he was going to bring her home tonight and claim her.

Their main courses finished, the waitress returned and set down two plated slices of strawberry cheesecake in front of them. Diesel made a face. His mind had been preoccupied, and he didn't realize he'd also ordered dessert. He watched Carina's eyes light up with delight as she ogled the thin slice, which was topped with whipped cream and a red drizzle.

Diesel pushed the plate aside. Sometimes he wished his feline shifter kind had the ability to taste sweet things, so he could feel the same kind of pleasure Carina clearly did. "Ugh."

Carina blinked. "You don't like *cheesecake?*"

"Eh, sweets aren't my thing."

"So why did you order it?"

He shrugged. "I guess I thought I'd change my mind." He slid the plate in her direction. "Want mine?"

She chewed her bottom lip as her eyes bounced between the two plates. "This is totally going to fuck up my weight," she said under her breath.

He smirked. "Then I guess that means we're going to be training extra hard on Monday, huh?"

"Are you intentionally trying to keep me from reaching my weight goals?"

"Of course not. But it'd be a shame to let such a delectable-looking slice of cheesecake go to waste, so..."

She smiled coyly at him then picked up her fork. "You're terrible. But I guess I gotta take the pain with the pleasure."

Her response sent a tingle to his groin. He narrowed his eyes, allowing his tiger to mull over her playful comment. *Pain, pleasure, I'll give you both if you want it.* "I think you should enjoy yourself for a change and splurge." *Then come home with me so you can have much more.*

She chuckled. "Well, since I have your blessing..." She cut a small piece and popped it in her mouth. A bit of whipped cream stuck to the corner of her mouth as she chewed.

Pain throbbed in his dick as he watched her, thinking of how he could cover much more than just her mouth in white cream.

Carina rolled her tongue across her lips, licking away the stray whipped cream. He watched her tongue and absently mimicked her. His inner beast growled with contentment, the sensation eventually reaching his throat.

She looked at him oddly. "You okay?"

He cleared his throat, attempting to ease his sensations and calm his tiger. "Yeah." He exhaled. "Come home with me tonight."

"W-What?" Her voice cracked.

"You heard me."

She pursed her lips.

"What are you afraid of?" he insisted.

"I..."

"Is it because I'm your trainer? That I can't separate business from pleasure?"

She fidgeted with the hem of the tablecloth. "No. I don't want to end up falling for you and... and we ruin a good thing."

He quirked a smile. *She's falling for me.* He let out a soft, throaty growl of approval, and took her hands in his. "If you fall for me, nothing will be ruined."

She stared at their hands. "But, my car..."

"We'll take my car. I promise to bring you back."

"But..."

He stared at her face intently, waiting for an answer.

She moistened her lips and thought for a moment, then met his gaze. "Okay."

Grinning, Diesel gestured to the waitress for the bill. The waitress returned with an itemized receipt in a leather-bound check holder. Apparently, they'd eaten a lot less than five hundred dollars' worth. He was still annoyed at Cammy's meddling, even though her generous prank had worked in his favor.

Cammy... Diesel ground his teeth and checked his phone. He'd missed a message from her earlier while he and Carina were enjoying their dinner. Scowling, he was ready to give her a piece of his mind when he read Cammy's message:

Cam: ffs, claim her already!!! @_@

Diesel fought a small smile that crept back across his lips. She knew. Somehow, she knew. He didn't smell his sister nearby, but she seemed to know more about himself than he did.

The waitress returned, and he handed her back the folio.

"Keep the rest as the tip," he told her, and her face lit up brighter than the sun. She would most likely be getting the best tip of the night to match Diesel's generous mood. Because tonight, he intended to give Carina everything.

CHAPTER 12

Diesel sped on the highway with the convertible top down, not caring how much he went over the speed limit. His tiger needed attention from the beautiful curvy woman sitting in the passenger seat.

"This is surreal," Carina said.

"What?" Diesel looked sideways.

"This... *date*."

"Oh, so it's a date now?" He flashed her an amused grin.

"I guess it is."

"You don't sound too sure of yourself."

"I just never thought I'd experience dating again, and I never in a million years thought it would be *you*."

He snorted out a chuckle. "We can do it more if you want."

"Let's just see how tonight goes, eh?"

He leaned his arm out the driver's side window and enjoyed the cool evening breeze. It was a clear night with every star in full view. It was a perfect night, but Carina's doubts overshadowed the romantic mood. "What do you want in a man, 'Ri?"

Carina fell silent and looked thoughtful for a moment. "I've never been asked that before. I just want a man who will love me for who I am and won't play games with my heart. And he needs to love me long-term."

Check. Check. Che— "Long-term?" Diesel repeated, arching an eyebrow.

"Yes, you know. Settling down, getting married, having children. I'm thirty-five. Pretty soon, my dreams of being able to have a family will be gone. I've always wanted kids, but the men I've been with didn't want any part of that kind of life."

Her strong desire for children reminded him of the baby shower he was supposed to attend the next day. Carina's words made him want to spend the day with her making babies of their own. But backing out at the last minute would be a real dick move for him to do to Leah, especially after he'd promised he would come. And he was a man of his word. "I love a woman who knows exactly what she wants," he said to Carina.

"Oh? Is that all you want in a woman?" she asked in a coy tone.

He pondered her question as he took the exit ramp toward Hunter's Rest. "No. I also want a sexy, curvy woman I can settle down with. I want to treat her like the queen she is and spoil her to her heart's content because she deserves every ounce of my love. And I want to have many children with her."

She raised her eyebrows. "Many? How *many* were you thinking?"

"As many as she can handle."

She laughed and shook her head. "Children are a blessing, but too many can get overwhelming."

"If their mother is anywhere close to being an amazing woman like you, then it would never get overwhelming."

She turned her head away from him. He sensed he'd made her blush. Perhaps he'd finally begun chipping away at her icy wall of fear. Always a good sign.

He veered off the main road and onto a tree-lined private street. The lack of streetlights made the area pitch-black, but Diesel knew exactly where he was going.

"It's so dark. Where are we?" Carina asked.

He turned down a hidden gravel driveway. The moon cast a small glimmer over the roof of his two-bedroom, two-bathroom wood cabin, while the front porch light illuminated the entrance in a warm, welcoming glow. "Home." He parked at the entrance and got out of the car. He rounded the passenger's side and opened the door for Carina.

"What a cozy-looking cabin," she said, stepping out.

He took her hand and escorted her to the front door. "Just the way I like it."

"Are we still in New Rochford?

"No, this is Hunter's Rest, a small town in the mountains thirty miles north of the city. Come." He took her hand and led her inside. He left her in the main room for a moment while he disappeared into the kitchen.

"This is beautiful," he heard her say in a near-breathless tone as he poured two glasses of chardonnay.

He returned to the main room to find her sitting on the edge of the couch, ogling the wooden inset bookshelves that flanked the stone fireplace. He handed her a glass of wine and plopped down next to her on the couch.

"I've always loved cabin homes," Carina continued. "That feeling of nature and the outdoors... that unique cozy charm..."

"You like the outdoors?" He took a sip of his wine.

She nodded. "The outdoors can be liberating. Besides, I like a good long walk in the woods every now and then."

He made a mental note of that while he set his glass on a side table. They seemed to be already compatible on that front.

Carina took a long sip of her wine, then her gaze flicked to the large rug in the middle of the room. Unlike the pristine state of the rest of the room, the rug was shabby and ridden with tufts of orange-brown fur. But the carpet was so soft and comfortable, it was his favorite spot in his cabin to lounge while he was in his tiger form.

"Looks like that rug's seen better days," Carina said.

Diesel scratched the back of his head. "Damn, guess I forgot to vacuum again."

She raised her eyebrows. "You have a dog or something?"

He scoffed. "A dog! Absolutely not."

"Then where did all this hair come from?"

"It's mine."

"What?" She blinked. "Oh! You mean..." She suddenly laughed. "Oh my gosh. I can't believe all this time I've known you, I never knew you were a shifter."

"I don't go around announcing it like some people. I'd rather keep that sort of thing to myself. Sometimes you get the wrong attention from the wrong people, and I don't have time for that."

"The wrong people? As in other shifters?"

"Other shifters, those few groups of people who hate our kind, and those assholes who would treat you differently when they find out what you are. I don't have time for that bullshit, so I keep that part of my life private."

"Oh..." Carina frowned and swirled the contents of her glass. "I didn't realize shifters have it so rough."

He shrugged. "Being a shifter is like being any other magic-possessing person. We're different, and so you get those dickheads every now and then who don't like different."

"I get it." Carina nodded. Her frown disappeared, replaced with a playful smile. "So what are you? A dragon? A wolf?"

"A *wolf*?" he growled. "Seriously?"

"What? I think wolves are sexy."

"Oh, really?"

"So are you going to humor me and tell me what kind of shifter you are?"

He cast her a brief, intent stare then got up from the couch. "How about I show you instead." Approaching the hair-ridden rug, he undid his necktie and undressed himself. As soon as he'd stepped out of his pants and underwear, he heard a small gasp behind him. Smirking, he sprawled out naked on the rug. He closed his eyes and concentrated, calling forth his caged tiger. A greater strength encompassed him, and the muscles in his body grew and strengthened. His senses heightened, and the colors in his vision dulled to less-saturated hues. Striped, orange-brown fur grew over his skin. He let go of the remainder of his human consciousness, allowing his shifting to complete.

Carina almost dropped her wine glass but recovered her grip on the stem just in time. She set the glass on the side table next to his and sprang up from the couch. She stared at Diesel, her face a mix of awe and terror. "Oh shit! A tiger? The next best thing!"

Diesel growled. *The* next *best thing?* He intended to change her perception by the end of the night. He rested his chin on his paws and stared up at her insistently.

She bit her bottom lip and approached him slowly. "Um, may I touch you?"

That simple, innocent question sent a ripple of pleasure through his body, and he lashed his tail back and forth. For now, he would let her explore him, knowing that he would also be thoroughly exploring her soon enough.

She knelt before him. "Does that mean yes? Please don't bite me."

He narrowed his eyes in amusement. *Oh, there'll be lots of biting involved, my sweet tigress.*

She swallowed once then slowly extended her hand. Her fingers grazed the top of his head then continued down his back. Her touch soothed him.

He shut his eyes and welcomed her gentle strokes to the back of his neck, behind his ears, and under his chin.

"You're so beautiful. So soft," she murmured.

Letting out a contented growl, he nudged her hand and gave it a small lick. She started, most likely from his rough, sandpaper touch, but it was the only way he knew how to end the cute little foreplay. It was his turn. He closed his eyes and concentrated again, allowing the beast to sleep and assuming his human form once more. He sat before her as a naked man and fully aroused.

Her eyelids fluttered downward, and a blush appeared on her cheeks.

"Now that I got your attention..." He caressed the side of her face. "I want to explore *you* in much more depth."

Her breath hitched. He drew his face closer to hers. Her mouth opened, as though she wanted to say something, but he pressed his lips to hers before she had the chance. He felt her reciprocate the kiss, pressing her lips harder to his. She let out a small moan, and he knew he had her. She tasted far better than he'd imagined. And the smell of her need kept his tiger aware.

He crawled closer to her, and she backed away, laughing. *Oh, now she wants to play hard to get?* Grinning, he followed her. Finally, she backed herself against the couch. He closed in on her and pinned her there, running his fingers through her thick, curly hair. He slid his hands down, over her cheeks, her neck, and across her bare shoulders, then claimed her mouth while his hands explored her curves. Pressing her lips harder against his, Carina moaned with need. A shiver ran through his body.

His hands felt for the back zipper of her dress and gently tugged it down. The zipped-down dress gathered around her full hips and belly. He glanced down and grinned. As he looked back up to her face, he noticed her cringe and felt her body tense.

Damn, she's cute when she's embarrassed, he thought.

He gently guided his hands over her soft belly, relishing its contour. "Are you still worried about this?"

She squirmed at his touch. "Ugh, yes! Don't do that."

His hands caressed along her sides, and his fingers massaged every inch of her supple skin. "And these?"

She winced. "Yes! This is embarrassing."

"It doesn't need to be, and you shouldn't be so worried about your gorgeous, sexy body, either."

She exhaled deeply through her nose. "Easy for you to say, D."

"Even easier for me to show you." He helped her wriggle out of the dress then tossed it aside. He pinned every inch of her deliciously curvy body with his gaze. She turned her head away, avoiding his eye contact. He placed both hands on her cheeks and turned her head back, forcing her to look at him. "Don't *ever* be worried or ashamed. You are the sexiest woman I've ever laid eyes on, and tonight, I'm going to make you mine." He claimed her mouth with his then ran his tongue across her full lips. Feeling her body relax, he kissed down the length of her neck, his hands following in a gentle caress along her soft skin. His tongue flicked across her chest and down her sternum, getting lost in her cleavage. Her unique scent enveloped his senses and drove his tiger wild.

"Ah..." She shuddered then hissed.

His dick steeled at her body's reactions. He pulled back from his kiss, grabbed her bra by its center gore, and ripped off the garment. Her ample breasts bounced free. Her dark nipples were recessed, but he'd change that quickly.

"So gorgeous," he whispered, his tiger approving. He took one of her breasts in his mouth and sucked hard while he teased the other with his hand.

"Oh, fuck, D!" she gasped.

"Mmm…" His tongue swirled around until he felt her nipple pop out from hiding and harden to a pebble. Then he gave it gentle, playful flicks with his tongue. Her musky scent was getting stronger, and he had no doubt her black panties were soaked. But he would have his dessert later. For now, in his usual feline manner, his tiger was having too much fun playing with her. He wondered how many times he could make her cum tonight.

As he squeezed her breast with his hand, he sucked her harder until she let out a moan. He pressed down on her nipple with his tongue, then gently nipped and tugged it with his teeth. He flicked her other nipple with his thumb until it slowly protruded enough for him to pinch and tease with his fingers.

She cried out, her body quivering as she came undone. He inhaled her musk—it'd grown stronger—and smirked at her. *That's one.*

"Look at that. You came already. Such a good girl," he said with a smirk.

She bit her bottom lip. "I... I couldn't help it..."

He chuckled darkly. Of course she couldn't. She was at his mercy, and he was just getting started.

He explored her body further, his hands moving down to her sides, his fingers getting lost in her ample flesh. He kissed all over her belly and slid his tongue along every soft curve.

"Oh, hell, don't kiss there. Why do you have to kiss *there?*" she whimpered.

He squeezed and kneaded her sides. "Because I love your body. You're so grabbable. So soft. So perfect." He rubbed his hands over her belly and kissed it more passionately. "Get used to having a big belly, my dear. Because I'm going to keep it full of cubs."

"Damn." She shuddered. "I can't possibly have that many."

"And why not? It's what we both want, yes?"

"I said I wanted kids, but..."

"Then we'll make it happen." He moved his hands across her thighs and spread her legs. He tore off those damned panties—fully soaked, as he'd expected—with a single tug and tossed the useless garment with the rest of her discarded clothes. He adored the sight of her pussy, drenched in her addictive scent that drove his tiger crazy. "But first, I want to taste every bit of you."

He trailed his fingers along her pussy, getting them coated in her juices, then licked his fingers. "Mmm..."

"Ugh, don't do that." She looked away, her face turning a deeper shade of red.

He licked the remnants of her juice from his lips. "You're too damn delicious for me *not* to." He lifted her hips, letting her thick thighs rest on his broad shoulders, and he buried his face into her pussy, eating her out with his tongue.

"Shit! D!" she cried.

Her body trembled as he drove his tongue as deep as he could inside then swirled it along her walls, tasting every drop of her juice. She tasted better than the finest wine. He glided his tongue across her clit, flicking it repeatedly, and then he sucked on her little pink pearl. She tried to squirm, but he pinned her in place with his weight. As he gently nibbled on her clit, he heard her cries turn to screams, and something hot suddenly touched his tongue. *At last.* Eager to taste her addicting nectar again, he prodded his tongue inside her, stimulating her core. Her body contracted, and he hungrily devoured every drop of her orgasm. *That's two.* He growled in satisfaction.

"You came again," he murmured.

"Please, I... I can't... My legs... so weak..." she croaked between breaths.

He guided her hips and pulled her to him. Her pussy, already nice and wet, accommodated his throbbing dick as he slid inside her easily. He exhaled, focusing on her with narrowed eyes, as he fought to maintain control of his tiger. Fought the temptation to shift, otherwise he'd break her.

She shut her eyes, and her face contorted with a mix of emotions as he rocked her hard and drove deeper. Her mouth open, she cried his name over and over. Holding on to her hips, he quickened his thrusts until he felt his dick reach her hot center.

"Please..." she whispered, her voice cracked.

He felt her walls clamp his dick. Her shaky hands reached up to his head, her fingers getting lost in his hair. His throbbing dick drove in and out of her, harder, faster. He felt himself losing control as he drew closer to his release. His grip on his humanity was slipping.

"Cum for me again," he ordered.

She moaned. "Again? I… can't…"

"You can, and you will." Growling, he forcefully rolled her onto her stomach. She whimpered and braced herself with shaky arms on the couch. He grabbed her hips, pulling her harder into his thrusts. His fingers dug into her skin, his nails just long and sharp enough to puncture flesh. The smell of her sex tinged with a hint of blood sent him over the edge. His dick pulsed against her cervix, and his body tensed. The colors around him went dull. With a mighty roar, he released, filling her up with his seed. Her screams ripped through the air, and he felt the walls of her pussy constrict his dick tighter, milking him for all he had. His dick was bathed in another round of her hot orgasm.

That's three.

"That's a good girl," he purred in her ear, then feathered a kiss on her cheek. His body shuddered as he thrust in and out of her, riding his orgasmic high as his animal instincts took over. He withdrew briefly and muttered, "Now I'm going to claim you."

She panted then slowly opened her eyes. "C-claim..." she whimpered.

"We will be bonded for life."

She chewed her bottom lip. "Like marriage?"

"Not quite, but less complicated. I desire only you, Carina, my tigress. I want you as my mate."

She let out a sigh, and her body relaxed. "A mate... Is... Is this a dream?"

He let out a low, guttural growl, sliding his hands up from around her hips to caressing her belly. He pressed his hips against her big, luscious ass, driving his thick cock back into her for another round. "It is not a dream," he murmured.

She trembled, a loud cry escaping her. "D... I'm so numb... I can't take anymore..."

He sank his teeth into his bottom lip, relishing her passionate plea. "Then tell me to stop."

"Nngh... Uhh..."

He gave her another thrust. "Hmm?"

"Ahh..."

His dick pulsated against her walls, ready to explode another load of his seed. His breath hitched as he held back for her just a little while longer. "Tell me you'll be my mate," he growled in her ear.

She exhaled and groaned. "Oh, fuck..."

"Tell me." One of his hands wandered back to her breast.

"Ugh... I never thought it'd ever be you," she said in one breath.

"Tell me," he repeated, his voice between a mix of human and animal. His tiger was on edge again, yearning to fuck her to oblivion. His fingers found her pebble-hard nipple. He twisted and tugged on it while he continued grinding his dick into her, and she squirmed in response.

"Ahh! Yes, D! Yes! I'll be your mate!" she screamed.

Beaming at her affirmation, he slowly drew his lips from her ear. "Good girl." He licked down her neck to her upper back, tasting the sweat and lust on her smooth skin. Both of his hands returned to her hips, and he pulled her against him, driving his dick a few more inches deeper inside her. A low growl rumbled in his throat, and he buried his canines into the nape of her neck, marking her as his, finishing the deed.

Mine.

Smiling, he licked her delectable blood from the wound until it closed.

Her body twitched, and her screams came out as hoarse cries. Another hint of warmth touched his throbbing dick as she came fiercely. *That's four.* The feel of her climax set him over the edge, and he let loose another round of his pent-up seed into her, until it began to seep out of her vagina and drizzle down her inner thighs like melted ice cream.

"Such a good fucking girl," he whispered. His satisfied tiger returned to its slumber, and he finally collapsed on top of her, his dick still pulsating inside her while he savored the afterglow. Carina slumped against the edge of the couch, closed her eyes, and steadied her exhausted breathing. Diesel listened to his fast-beating heart against her back.

"You're amazing," he said, kissing her ear.

She smiled weakly, not opening her eyes. "Am I?"

"Yes. I made you cum four times."

"Huh. That's a first for me." She let out a weak laugh.

"You still think wolves are sexier than tigers?"

"Oh no. *Hell* no."

CHAPTER 13

Carina thought she had been dreaming, but her weak legs, sore back and pussy, and over-sensitive nipples told her otherwise. She was glad to be back at her home late Saturday morning to recover from the wild night with Diesel. How the hell did she even let it get that far? She couldn't remember the last time she'd had good dick in her. And *damn,* was he good. Too good. Just thinking about having him inside her again made her pussy tingle. It seemed the more she tried to deny him, the more attracted he was to her. And after what he'd told her at dinner, and at his cabin, she was convinced that he wasn't like her past men. Diesel did strange things to her that she couldn't understand. He was drawn to her like bee to a rose. She was falling for this tiger-man hard and fast.

After all, she'd let him claim her. The pain on her neck was a constant reminder of the most erotic feeling she'd ever experienced. She couldn't think of another person she would want to spend the rest of her life with other than Diesel. A man who seemed to truly love her for who she was and not for her looks. Maybe Cammy was the good luck charm she needed. Carina hoped one day she'd see the carefree young woman again.

A nice cold shower calmed Carina's nerves, and she stepped out of the bathroom feeling refreshed. But her body was still in pain. She couldn't remember much from that moment with him, only that he'd gone feral with lust, fucking her pussy more times than she could count. She ran her hand across the back of her neck and winced from a sharp pain. There was a fresh scab where she'd been bleeding. Damn, she'd been so aroused, she couldn't remember feeling pain until now. She treated the wound as best she could with ointment then got dressed.

With the weekend being reserved as rest days from the gym, Carina decided to do her weekly food run. On her way to the supermarket, she stopped at a traffic light. Recognizing the familiar intersection, she spotted Gauge's shop on the corner. Sparks showered down from under a car that was high up on a lift in one of the open bays. Gauge was hard at work again.

She pulled up to the supermarket, which was a block away from the mechanic shop. Her mind was a jumble of emotions while she shopped, and the longer she stayed out in public, the more anxious she became. She wasn't sure if the anxiety was for Diesel or the need to relieve herself of pent-up sexual tension.

With her head down, she left the supermarket with her bags in tow. She suddenly bumped into something solid, jarring her from her thoughts. Startled, she looked up.

Gauge stood before her in his mechanic's uniform, holding a wrapped sandwich from the supermarket's deli. He cast her one of his charming smiles that she couldn't resist. "Hi, again, Miss Carina."

She swallowed. He was sounding flirty, just like before. *Damn, do I really have two hot guys interested in me?* That possibility was a definite first time for her. "G-Gauge. Hi," she stammered.

He gestured to the bags. "Want me to help you with those?"

She shook her head. "No, thanks. I got it. What are you doing here?"

He held up his wrapped sandwich. "Lunch. Care to join me?"

"Well, actually, I have some things I need to take care of."

His smile faltered, a slight pinch in his brow appearing. He sniffed once, and his jaw tightened. "All right. Well, I hope we can get together sometime this weekend."

The irritation in his voice didn't go unnoticed. *Shit.* She was so caught up in Diesel's charms, she'd forgotten about their rain check. "We can still do that if you want. I don't go to the gym on the weekends."

"That's good. You should let your body rest sometime."

"Eh, I've got goals, but my personal trainer demanded I use the weekend to rest."

"Who's your trainer?"

"His name is Diesel. Diesel Reed. He's the gym owner."

Gauge scowled. "Diesel?"

"Yeah." She paused and studied him carefully. "You know, you kind of remind me of him."

His lip curled. "Impossible. We are *nothing* alike."

"You know him?"

His gaze shifted away from her face. "I know *of* him. Word of his... *deeds* gets out."

Her stomach did a flip. "What deeds?"

"Eh..." He scratched his shadow-bearded jaw in thought. "He's, uh, been known to steal others' mates and impregnate them, forcing them to either join his clan or die. He cares nothing about his mates, other than his excuse to call himself an alpha. But he is far, far from it. It sucks for all the women he's hurt."

Carina gasped. "W-What?" The world around her suddenly felt smaller.

Gauge nodded solemnly. "Be careful around him, all right? His reputation precedes him. He hides his true personality well in order to catch any woman in his charms. I mean, he must be pretty damn good-looking to be able to do that, y'know?"

But you're good-looking, too. "How do you know so much about him?"

"Because he's a tiger like me, and very few things go unnoticed in our community." He hardened his gaze at her. "I would hate to hear about a beautiful girl like you getting hurt by an asshole like him."

She chewed her bottom lip, many questions swarming in her mind. "Thank you for your concern. I'll be careful."

He sniffed again, and his lip curled a little. "Too late..." he muttered to himself.

"Huh?"

"Nothing, just thinking aloud. By the way, if you see him again, don't tell him about me, okay? He can get possessive if he finds out you've been talking to other men. I don't want you to get hurt."

Her heart thundered in her chest. "Uh... okay. I won't say anything."

"Good." His face brightened. "So, about that rain check... Why don't we do dinner tonight? There's this nice Italian place downtown."

Dinner... Perhaps taking Gauge's offer might be what she needed to get her mind straight. She was still indebted to him for fixing her car for free, after all. She didn't see the harm in having a casual dinner with him in return. "All right. Sounds good." She nodded. "I'm always down for Italian."

"Great, I'll call you later."

She watched him head back to his shop. Clutching the bags in her arms, she thought about her conversation with Gauge. Her stomach still turned as she thought about her wild night with Diesel. *Could D really be like that?*

"I desire only you, Carina, my tigress. I want you to be mine."

He desired *her*. His words had sounded so serious, so genuine.

And he'd *claimed* her.

But the more she thought about it, the more she wondered if last night was just a dream.

Or worse yet, a lie.

CHAPTER 14

Diesel could barely keep his eyes open on the road as he drove the long stretch of highway to the city. He was relieved that Cammy decided to leave him in peace today for a change and go sightseeing around the city with her hostel roommate instead. But with his anxiety over his little sister out of the way for a while, his mind kept drifting to Carina—and making her his mate. Thanks to Cammy's nudging, Diesel had taken the leap, and now he couldn't stop thinking about the future. A future with Carina. He had it all planned: she would rule by his side, and he would soon grow his clan. Then he could forget the days of his fuckups and becoming the family outcast, and he would start a new family of his own.

He gripped the wheel tighter, trying not to think of that day his eldest brother, Axle, had defeated him and became the new alpha.

"You have two options: leave or die," Axle had said as he stood over Diesel's defeated, wounded body on that fateful night of the duel.

Axle's words had sounded jumbled in Diesel's mind. The fierce battle scrambled his brain, and he was overwhelmed by the smell of his own blood. With his last bit of strength, Diesel returned to all fours and, with his tail between his legs, limped away from the only place he'd called home.

"There's no place for weakness," his younger brother, Gauge, had said, as Diesel walked away from home for the last time. Like Cammy, Gauge was a damn instigator. But unlike his sister, Gauge was bent on becoming the next alpha. He was kissing Axle's ass for the moment, but Diesel knew it wouldn't be long before Gauge tried to challenge Axle as well. And Diesel hoped Axle would lose so that smug look would be wiped off his face. In the meantime, Diesel would train his ass off to get stronger, wiser, and more prepared for the day that

he might have to face his brothers again—which he hoped was never.

"You have arrived at your destination." The voice from the GPS snapped Diesel back to the present. He glanced out the driver's window at an illuminated sign of a fancy wine glass, with *Bruschetta e Vino Ristorante* scrawled at the bottom in fancy script. When Leah told him she'd booked an Italian restaurant to host her baby shower, he didn't think she meant one of the most expensive, high-end restaurants in town. Not quite as expensive as Blue Iris Fusion, but it would easily make a close second on the list. Apparently, Leah hadn't changed a bit. She was as high-maintenance as her type came, and it seemed she planned to make sure her kid was the same way.

Not my *cubs.* He intended to make all of his children independent, self-sufficient warriors.

After parking his car, he grabbed his gift and headed inside the restaurant. The wait staff showed him to a private room at the back. Guests, all of them women, were already there. They looked his way and waved, smiling. He couldn't help but notice that most of the women lacked rings.

Damn. It was all making sense, him being the only man in a room full of single women. As he approached the table of gifts, he felt many eyes watching his every move.

"Diesel! You made it!" Leah chirped from behind him.

As he turned, Leah wrapped her arms around him in a tight hug. She pressed her body against his, and he felt the tight bump of her eight-month baby belly. He tensed, and his mind drifted to Carina in that moment, thinking about how beautiful it would be if she carried his children.

"Thank you for coming," Leah whispered in his ear.

He gently pulled out of her embrace and smiled politely. "Thanks for inviting me." He glanced around at the other women in the room, who were still eyeing him like he was fresh meat. "Any other guys coming?" he asked Leah.

She looked at him for a moment then laughed. "You're funny. But you're also cute, too. That's why I love you so much."

He made a face. He hated to hear that word thrown around haphazardly. "Love" was something he took seriously, and Leah was too into her own world to realize what she'd said. He could never love this woman as anything other than a friend, but the longer he remained around her, the more he felt even that friendship starting to fizzle. They led two different lives, and she'd started to mistake his kindness for weakness.

"You're just in time for dinner," Leah continued, gesturing to an empty seat at one of the round dining tables. "The gifts will be opened afterward."

He reluctantly slid into the seat and gave his tablemates a forced smile, but he cared nothing about those women vying for his attention. His thoughts remained on Carina. *If only I could speed up time.*

Carina glanced up from her phone to the lighted sign above the Italian restaurant and wondered if she was at the right address that Gauge had texted her. The *Bruschetta e Vino Ristorante* was one of the top five-star restaurants downtown. Seemed like overkill for a casual rain check. Had Gauge realized that before he'd booked the reservation?

While she stressed over whether or not her green sundress was below standards for the restaurant, a black motorcycle pulled up beside the curb. A man in a muscle-defining, grey collared dress shirt and black slacks suit dismounted and slipped off his helmet.

Gauge's short brown hair was slicked back, accentuating a chiseled jawline with a shadow of beard. He locked his gaze on her and approached, giving her a smile that could charm the panties off any woman. "Glad you made it. I hope you didn't have any problems finding the place."

"No, but I wasn't expecting us to eat at one of the most expensive restaurants in town," Carina said. "Don't you think this is a little too much? I feel so underdressed..."

He laughed. "You didn't know about the rooftop lounge?" He pointed toward the roof of the three-story building. White Christmas lights were strung from the railing that lined the rooftop. Mellow jazz music, laughter, and chatter filtered from the small groups of people that gathered above.

She followed his gaze. She'd never officially eaten at that restaurant, only passed by it every day on her way home from work. "They have food up there?"

"Yeah. It's all part of the restaurant. All the fancy shit is on the main floor. The rooftop is where it's at. We can not only still eat in style, but we can also enjoy some live music, and a nice view of the city.

Her body relaxed and she smiled. "That sounds like fun."

"Of course it is. And it only took the new guy in the neighborhood to show you." He flashed her a cheeky smile.

"Hey, I may be a local, but I don't go out to places like this often. Never had a reason to."

"Well, now you do." He winked at her.

She gave him a curious look then let out an airy laugh. His charms intrigued her, and she always loved a man who could make her laugh and smile—a trait that Diesel didn't fully have. But Diesel's mysteriousness and overall sex appeal more than made up for that.

Gauge took her hand, and they walked inside the restaurant's lobby. Carina glanced around the dimly lit, rustic-style interior of the main area. A grand piano sat in the middle of the large room, where patrons at nearby tables had a full view of the musical entertainment.

A waiter stood at a podium in front of the entrance to the main room, but Gauge led Carina to a gold-trimmed elevator off to the side. Gauge called the elevator with a push of a button, and it opened moments later. The elevator's interior glowed with a soft, calming blue light. Gauge pushed the illuminated button for the third floor, which had a small gold plate etched with the word 'Lounge.'

The elevator zoomed up to the third floor and the doors opened to a grand, picturesque view of the lighted, busy main street of Grandway Square Boulevard, outlined by hanging ivy and other flora attached to the lounge's walls and along the railing. Soft jazz music played from a male trio set up in a corner. Two suited waiters meandered about, tending to the patrons. A large bar occupied the back of the lounge, where several patrons sat around on high stools. A young woman bartended the drinks, her hands working autonomously as she gathered, mixed, and served her latest concoction to each waiting customer.

Some of the patrons were dressed in their finest suits and dresses, but most wore casual slacks, skirts, halter tops, polos, and other general nightclub attire. Suddenly, Carina didn't feel so underdressed.

Gauge ushered Carina to an empty table near the railing. Gauge helped her into her chair before seating himself. Carina couldn't stop ogling the well-dressed couples and the romantic atmosphere that practically eclipsed last night's awkward dinner date with Diesel. Her gaze followed a woman who got up from a nearby table and headed toward the elevator with her male companion. The sequins on her red silk dress glittered like tiny stars.

"You like merlot?"

Gauge's voice suddenly shook her back to the present, and she acknowledged him with a pinched brow. "Merlot?"

"You know... wine? To drink?" He gave her a baffled look.

"Oh, right. Of course. Yes, that's fine."

He called one of the wandering waiters over and ordered two glasses.

Carina sank in her chair and stared at the menu that the waiter had set in front of her. *I'd better figure out what I want to eat before my mind wanders off again.*

"You don't seem to be all there tonight," Gauge said. "You still want to be here?"

Carina looked up from the menu. "What? Of course I do. I'm sorry, I just had a busy day today."

The waiter returned with their wine and took their food orders. Gauge and Carina made a small toast to their friendship. As Carina took a sip of her wine, she stared blankly toward the city lights.

He looked at her carefully. "You talk to Diesel lately?"

Her heart stopped at the mention of his name, and she fixed her gaze on Gauge. "Not today. Why?"

He shrugged. "Just worried about you, it's all. He knows how to pull on girls' heartstrings. Certain reputations are not exactly secret in our society. You act like an asshole, and everyone knows it."

She fidgeted with a tiny loose string on the black tablecloth. She'd made it clear to Diesel what she wanted. Hell, she'd let him *claim* her! She didn't want to believe that last night was just a whim. A quick one-night stand. His way of sampling her goods then tossing her aside. She was no stranger to that sort of treatment, but she swore she wouldn't get herself into that situation again.

After she'd taken those boudoir shots, she'd begun to feel a little more confident in herself. She'd begun at night, before bed, to stare at her photos, and remind herself—as Autumn had reminded her—that she *was* a queen.

But even queens sometimes had doubts which clouded their mind, and hers was in the form of Diesel.

"I had dinner with him the other night," Carina replied to Gauge at last. "It was nice." She left it at that.

Gauge nodded, looking convinced enough to not prod any further. "Just don't settle. A beautiful woman like you deserves only the best. Too bad Diesel's other women weren't so lucky."

She frowned, making a mental note to confront Diesel about Gauge's accusations.

The waiter set down Carina's dinner plate and uncovered it, revealing piping-hot chicken piccata. While everything looked and smelled delicious, her appetite was shot, thanks to her racing thoughts. She slowly picked up her fork and forced herself to eat a few bites.

"I know it's him," Gauge said.

She blinked out of her thoughts. "What?"

He rolled his eyes. "Don't fool yourself. You're smitten. But do you think he's willing to fight for you?"

She bit her bottom lip. "I don't know…"

"If you have doubts, then maybe he's not worth your time and stress."

Maybe Gauge was right, but she couldn't simply shake off her feelings for Diesel. She couldn't take back the fact that she'd bonded with him. That he'd marked her. What would their bonding mean if Diesel no longer desired her? She wanted to enjoy this night with Gauge, but it seemed her mind—and her heart—didn't want her to have that satisfaction.

Her thoughts and worries agitated that sharp pain in the back of her neck. "Ugh!" She winced, rubbing the spot.

Gauge gave her a concerned look. "Are you all right?"

"Yeah, I, uh… cut myself the other day. Not sure how it happened."

He arched an eyebrow. "You cut yourself?"

She nodded quickly. Her heart began to pound at his questioning look. "It was an accident, of course. I just don't remember how it happened. Where's the ladies' room?"

A small crease appeared at his brow. "Downstairs."

She got up from her chair. "I'm going to go to check on it. I'll be right back."

His eyes narrowed slightly, and he gave a small nod.

She pushed the button to the elevator, but it didn't come right away. She could feel Gauge's laser-stare burning into her back. Finally, she gave up and took the stairs. She descended the stairwell as fast as her platform heels would allow, until she arrived at the second-floor landing. The stairwell opened to a small hallway of three separate rooms that were closed off by French doors. One of the rooms—the one closest to the elevator—had a Reserved sign sitting out front. Two women wearing red and black dresses stood in front of the doors like bouncers. Carina wondered what special event was going on beyond.

The elevator next to the stairwell dinged, and a woman wearing an expensive-looking yellow dress stepped out, carrying a wrapped gift and balloons that said, "It's a girl!"

Carina blinked. *A baby shower.* Babies were the last thing she wanted to think about after what Gauge had told her about Diesel. She regretted getting caught up in Diesel's charms. *What if I'm pregnant?* She and Diesel hadn't taken any precautions, after all.

The yellow-clad woman approached the Reserved room. The two female bouncers smiled and chatted with her briefly, then let her in.

As Carina proceeded to the ladies' room, she heard muffled cheers and awes coming from the Reserved room. The female bouncers out front peered through the glass of the French doors and exchanged grins.

"She must've opened up Tori's gift," one of them chortled to the other.

Carina caught a glimpse of the crowded room beyond. A woman, who appeared to be very pregnant, wore a diamond tiara and sat in a makeshift throne that was surrounded by other women, pink balloons, and wrapped gifts.

"Excuse me. Move along. This is a private party," one of the female guards said, giving Carina a dismissive gesture with her hand.

Carina frowned. As she was about to continue to the ladies' room, she spotted something else. She narrowed her eyes as she glimpsed through the glass from afar. *Wait. Is that...*

Standing next to the pregnant queen, handing her a pink wrapped gift, was the last person Carina had hoped to see.

CHAPTER 15

DIESEL HAD NEVER BEEN SO bored in his life. *This is the last time I do a favor for a friend.* As he'd feared, no other men had arrived, and he was tasked with being the "gift distributor and eye candy" for all the women's amusement.

Leah was a piece of work. She sat on a fucking throne with a diamond crown, like the queen she thought she was. For the past thirty minutes, he'd been standing next to her like some idiot court jester, handing her gifts from the endless mountain of shit that all her prissy friends showered her with.

Damn it. He should've known better than to get caught up in Leah's charms. That's what he got for trying to be a good guy.

Leah unwrapped yet another gift, a pink hairband with diamonds and a matching diamond-studded pacifier. Diesel wasn't sure if they were real diamonds or not, but it looked expensive as hell, regardless.

For fuck's sake. This kid's going to be eating from a silver spoon. He handed Leah the next gift. As if fate were listening to his thoughts, she unwrapped an actual silver spoon.

He blinked. *Ho-ly shit.*

Leah clapped her hands. "Oh! It's absolutely adorable! My little Najia will love it!" She and the other women chortled with delight, sounding like a bunch of cackling hens.

He winced. There were still two hours and many more unwrapped presents to go. He sighed and handed her the next gift, trying to plaster on a polite smile.

As Leah took the gift from him, she grinned mischievously and turned to her friends. "Before I open the next gift, can we give our handsome distributor a round of applause for being such a good sport? Diesel has been such a great friend and personal trainer, helping me to get in shape and feel great about myself."

The women clapped, whistled, and cheered. He hated the attention, but he acknowledged the women with a small wave. He kept silent, for fear of prolonging this ridiculous party any more than it would otherwise last.

"Oh, and by the way, ladies, last I checked, he was still single," she added with a smirk and a wink.

Diesel shuddered. *Fucking really?* That brought on another wave of awes and fawning that he wished would end. As if the women weren't riled up enough.

"For real?" one of the women asked then chuckled. "Damn, I wanna be revved up by your diesel engine." The other women laughed.

Diesel rolled his eyes and sighed, resisting the urge to facepalm instead. From the time he and his siblings were born, they had heard every dry car joke in the book. A curse for having an eccentric father who was also a car enthusiast and die-hard gearhead.

"We need to talk after the party," another woman said. "I'm running on empty and I need you to fill me up."

A wave of catcalls filled the room. Diesel gently nudged Leah, urging her to open the next gift so the attention would shift away from him. While Leah continued, he let his mind wander. It was the only thing he could do to overcome this boredom. He wondered what Carina was doing, then he thought of what he would rather be doing to her, alone in his bed.

He noticed two of Leah's prissy friends standing outside like a couple of security guards. *Ridiculous.* No one in their right mind would give two shits about this over-the-top embarrassment of a party.

If only he could escape. If only he could see Carina again. If only...

A third woman came into view in the distance beyond the glass doors. He blinked. *Carina?*

Her face full of pain, Carina stared right back at him as though she were staring into his soul. The two women shooed Carina away, then shook their fingers at her in a scolding manner, saying something that Diesel's acute tiger hearing couldn't discern beyond the other women's loud voices in the room.

"Keep 'em coming, handsome!" Leah chirruped, and the other women giggled.

Wincing, he handed her another box but remained focused on the doors. *That couldn't have been Carina, could it?* He couldn't detect her scent, thanks to this room being full of all sorts of eye-watering perfumes.

His curiosity was piqued, and his tiger wouldn't let it rest until he knew for certain. He turned to Leah, who unwrapped a box of frilly dresses and onesies—probably the least expensive gift he'd seen, but knowing her friends, it probably cost more than a penthouse.

"Hey, I, uh... need to take a piss. Can I go do that?" he muttered to her.

She rolled her eyes and sighed. "Oh fine. Spoil the fun, why don't you? Hurry up. You've been the life of the party." She turned to her friends. "Sorry, girls. A brief intermission while our eye candy takes a potty break."

Her friends groaned.

Diesel bit his tongue, resisting the urge to tell all these women off for humiliating him. But for the moment, he was free, and he wasn't about to fuck up the window of opportunity. "Right. I'll be back."

He tore out of the room and didn't look back. He nearly bumped shoulders with one of the female guards outside and apologized, but he was more worried about where Carina had run off to. He immediately picked up her strong scent; she was definitely there. Perhaps she went to the bathroom. Or maybe she was upstairs at the rooftop lounge. Questions turned in his mind. Had she come to the restaurant alone? It wasn't exactly a singles' hangout.

"Coming back, right?" one of the female guards asked.

"Yeah, sure," he said absently, not looking at her. He waited a beat, hoping Carina would exit the women's bathroom, but when she didn't, he headed for the stairs. "I'm, uh… going to use the bathroom downstairs 'cause the men's is out of order," he informed the guards.

They shrugged and waved him off. "Hurry back!"

He made a beeline for the stairwell and headed upstairs to the lounge instead. He scanned the patrons from afar, observing every face. Carina was nowhere to be seen.

Next, Diesel headed down to the main lobby. If Carina was near, she'd probably come through here at some point. He just hoped that he would run into her soon.

A hint of a familiar scent suddenly caught his senses—a scent from the past. It lingered a little in the lobby, then drifted to the exit. As he was about to investigate, the elevator behind him dinged. The doors opened, and Carina appeared, wearing a cute green dress. She spotted him and paled like a frightened rabbit.

He smiled, but concern still haunted his mind. "Ri? Surprised to see you here."

She pursed her lips. "Likewise. Gotta go now. Talk to you later." She brushed past him, toward the exit doors and peered out the glass. "What the hell?" she muttered, a troubled look adorning her face.

Diesel approached her, his brow scrunched. "What's wrong?"

"I'm just looking for someone..." She craned her neck, looking back and forth out of the glass door. Then she muttered under her breath, "Did he just..."

He? Diesel stiffened. He took her hand. "Hey..."

"Excuse me." She snatched her hand away, opened the door, and left.

Frowning, he followed her. As he left the restaurant, he caught the other familiar scent again, no longer masked by the food and people inside the building. The scent was similar to his own, but it was still faint. Narrowing his eyes, Diesel scanned the area. Paranoia crept in his mind, and he wondered if what he smelled was real, or if his senses were tricking him.

"I can't believe this," Carina grumbled, standing by the curb. "This was supposed to be a quiet, stress-free night, and he ditches me!"

Diesel looked at her carefully. This couldn't be what he thought it was. She was his mate. Would she dare betray their bond? To his relief, he did not smell the other scent on Carina, but his body still tensed. He knew who the scent belonged to, and he couldn't believe his past had finally found him. His suspicions of Carina getting involved in his former family's affairs caused the hairs on the back of his neck to straighten. "Who ditched you?" he finally asked, hoping to get a straight answer from her.

Carina huffed. "What does it matter to you? It probably wouldn't be long until you did the same to me, too."

He blinked. "What?"

"Are you gonna honestly fuck with me like that? I knew we shouldn't have gone out last night.

Everything is ruined. After I told you about my previous bad relationships, you decide to add salt to the wound, doing this shit."

He exhaled, trying to make sense of her accusations. "Whoa. Hold on. I don't know what you're talking about."

She shook her head, her eyes getting glassy. "What did that 'bonding' really mean? Was it just your way to play with my emotions? Am I just another desperate girl to you? Another checkmark on your list? Huh?"

Things were going south faster than he could blink. *Where in the hell did she get these ridiculous allegations?* "Hey, you need to calm down." He reached out for her shoulder, but she slapped his hand away and shook her head.

"Don't touch me. I'm tired of lies. I'm tired of relationships. I'd rather be alone."

He growled and threw his hands up in exasperation. "Look, I've had one hell of a shitty day today. I'd like to know what the fuck I did to deserve this."

She snorted. "A shitty day? Being surrounded by all those beautiful fawning women?"

He perked up. "Wait, so is that what this is about?" *Is she... jealous?*

"I don't know. You tell me!"

"I was invited to a baby shower. I wish I hadn't come. It was the most boring party ever. And those 'fawning' women are terrible. I wouldn't be caught dead with any of them. Believe me." His phone suddenly buzzed in his pocket, startling him. Growling, he pulled it out and took a quick glance.

A text from Leah:

Leah: Get your sweet ass back here!
　　　The girls are waiting. ;)

He shuddered and switched his phone to silent mode. He could deal with Leah's drama later. Much later. He returned his attention to Carina.

Her arms folded, she pinned him with a hard stare. "It's hard to believe anything anymore, D," she said. "The one person I thought I could open my heart to ends up pulling the rug out from under me."

He huffed. He thought they were making great progress before. When did she start having doubts again? "I don't know why you suddenly stopped trusting me, but whatever else you've seen or heard obviously isn't what it seems. I couldn't wait to leave that damn baby shower. Bunch of prissy snoots who think their shit don't stink. My *acquaintance*, the mother-to-be, invited me. She was one of my old clients a while back, so I was simply giving her the courtesy of attending the party for her very first child. I had no idea that she was going to go as over-the-top as she did and rope me into being the "gift-giving eye candy" for all her cackling, stuck-up friends."

Carina glared at him, not seeming to buy his story.

He threw his hands up. "It's the fucking truth! I swear!"

Her face remained stony. Suddenly, she snickered then burst out laughing. "I can't believe you were actually coerced into attending a baby shower."

He blinked, her reaction throwing him. "Hey, it's not like I go to them on a daily basis. Besides, I was *trying* to be the nice guy doing a favor for a friend."

"Didn't you think to ask if you were going to be the only guy there?"

"Uh, no? Was I supposed to ask her who was on the guest list?"

Carina rolled her eyes and smiled. "Wow, you really are a virgin."

He bristled. "I'm most certainly *not* a virgin."

"A virgin for attending *baby showers*, D!"

"Oh..."

Her face softened, and she shook her head. "All right. I guess your situation sounds too farfetched to *not* believe. I'm sorry I overreacted."

"It's all right. Mistakes happen. But you still haven't told me your story. What are you doing at a fancy place like this?"

She sighed. "Like I said before, I was ditched. It was supposed to be a casual dinner. Gauge seemed pretty nice, until he—"

Diesel froze, his brother's name resonating in his mind, confirming his suspicions about the familiar scent. "Gauge?" he spat.

"He never told me his last name, but..." She paused, and her brow creased. "...wait, why are you looking like that?" She paused again and her eyes grew wide. "Oh shit. Do you know him?"

"Was he my height? Brown hair? Had tiger-striped tattoos on his right arm?"

She paled and chewed her bottom lip. "Y... Yes..."

"Then, yeah. That is Gauge Reed." He narrowed his eyes. "My brother."

CHAPTER 16

GAUGE. FUCKING *GAUGE* HAD TO add the final cherry on top of Diesel's sucktacular night. He wanted to believe that it was a dream, that Gauge and Carina were *not* here at this restaurant on a date.

Not after the intense night that Diesel and Carina had.

The shocked, jaw-dropping look on Carina's face explained everything. "Brothers! Oh, shit…"

"That's right. What were you doing here with him?" Diesel snapped.

She appeared confused a moment then closed her eyes and shook her head, as if trying to gather her thoughts. "Gauge fixed my car the other day.

He wanted to hang out this weekend, so we decided on a casual dinner and drinks at this place. I had no idea he was your brother. Why are you getting upset with me? Nothing serious is going on between me and Gauge."

"You're my mate."

She frowned. "And you forbid me to live my life because of it?"

"No. But because we have bonded, there may be others—rivals—who would dare try to take you away from me."

"Including your own brother?"

"*Especially* my own brother." He paused and took a deep breath. Exhaling through his nose, he tried to calm his agitated beast. "Look, whatever that bastard has told you, don't believe him."

She threw her hands up and shook her head. "Honestly? I don't know who or what to believe anymore. I feel like such an idiot right now. I just want to go home." She spun and headed for her car.

Diesel ran after her. "Wait."

She kept walking. "Leave me alone, D."

He wanted to stop her from leaving, but she was too headstrong. But if Gauge was after her, it could mean trouble. "Gauge is cunning and dangerous in his own right. At least let me follow you home and make sure you get there safely."

She reached her car and yanked open the driver's door. "Look, whatever. Just stay the hell away from me. I'm done tonight."

He exhaled a long sigh as he watched her speed off. His phone buzzed again with another message from Leah:

Leah: Where r u????

Sneering, he ignored the text and stuffed the phone back in his pocket. The safety of his mate from his unhinged brother was his highest priority. Leah and her group of cackling hens would be fine without him. *Good riddance.*

Diesel rushed across the street, hopped in his car, and followed Carina. He stayed far enough behind her to keep her distant taillights in view. Growling, he gripped the steering wheel tight and let his troubled mind wander.

First Cammy pays a visit, now Gauge... who else from the clan is here? he wondered. *Did Cammy bring Gauge here?* That idea sounded ridiculous since Cammy hated Gauge like the plague. Maybe Gauge put her up to it somehow.

He pushed a button on his steering wheel and activated his phone. "Call Cammy," he ordered the computerized system, not taking his eyes off the road.

"Calling Cammy," a robotic female voice echoed from the door speakers. The phone rang a few times and moments later, someone picked up.

"Hey, Big Brother!" Cammy greeted in a bubbly tone. "Did you go on another date with Carina today? I saw on my FindMe app that you were at some fancy restaurant. How was it? And what happened last night with you and Carina? Spill the deets!"

"Shut the fuck up!" Diesel barked, tightening his grip on the steering wheel. He made a mental note to add Cammy to his Blocked list on his FindMe app after he ended the call. "*I'm* asking the questions now. Why the hell is Gauge here?"

There was a brief pause. "What?" Cammy asked in a deflated tone.

"You heard me. Is that why you really came to see me? Did Gauge put you up to this in order to get to me?"

"I don't know what you're talking about. I have no idea why that furball is here."

Diesel snarled. "Stop lying! I'm not stupid."

"D, I swear, I know nothing about Gauge being here. Please believe me."

"No, that begging tone's not gonna work this time. Who else from the clan is coming here? Axle? Maybe he's here already, and you're just not telling me. What the fuck are you planning, Cammy? Tell me the truth!"

"D!" Cammy snapped back, her voice tinged with a growl. "For the last time, I have *nothing* to do with Gauge. I came here on my own to get away from Gauge, Axle, and the rest of the clan's shit. And I really wanted to see you for my birthday. If you don't believe me, well, that's your problem. But don't call me anymore harassing me about it."

He ground his teeth. It wasn't often he'd heard his sister talk seriously. Even through the phone, he could hear her tiger's agitation. For someone who always loved having a good time, making a joke of everything, not much set her off like this.

Conceding, Diesel pursed his lips and exhaled a long sigh through his nose. His angry tiger settled, and he refocused his thoughts. "I think Gauge is trying to get to me somehow. I don't know why."

"Why now? He never gave a fuck about you before," Cammy said.

"I don't know. I just… have this feeling. I bumped into Carina at the restaurant today. He apparently was with her at some point."

"What! He tried to steal your mate?"

"Yeah. But he ran off like a scared bitch, and stood Carina up on their little 'date.' Anyway, I'm making sure she gets back to her house safely, then I'm gonna search high and low for Gauge." He pulled up along the curb in front of an eleven-story, brick high-rise apartment building. A tarnished plated sign posted above the building's entrance read, 'Sinew Gardens Apartments.'

"My roomie's driving. We'll be where you are in ten minutes," Cammy said.

Diesel blinked. *How did she—* He paused and realized he hadn't yet blocked her from that tracking app. Then he wondered if Gauge was tracking him the same way, too. But they didn't have each other's phone numbers, so it was impossible for Gauge to track him. "No, I'll take care of Gauge," Diesel told his sister. "This is my problem. I'm not gonna drag you into it."

"Gauge is my brother, too. Therefore, he is also my problem. So I have every right to kick his ass as I see fit."

His lips hinted at a smile. Even in dark times, Cammy knew how to make light of a situation and calm his tiger. "Just stay out of this, please. I have to go now." He ended the call before she had a chance to respond. Then he blocked Cammy in FindMe, and shut off the app.

He stared back at the apartment building. He had never been to Carina's home before, as he'd stuck to his decision about not visiting clients, as tempting as it sometimes was. Carina lived in a nice neighborhood on a street that wasn't too busy. That brought some relief to him.

Carina turned onto a ramp that descended into the building's underground parking garage.

He checked his rearview and side mirrors to make sure he wasn't being followed, and then drove down the garage ramp. Dozens of cars packed like sardines occupied the first sub-level. Diesel spied Carina's car whip around a corner to the second sub-level, which ended in a short dead end. A single caged light affixed to the concrete wall cast its hazy amber glow in the area. Carina parked in an empty space along the wall. He backed into a space across from her and shut off the engine.

Carina got out of her car and pinned him with a cold stare from across the way. "I told you to leave me alone, D!"

He didn't get out of his car. "I'm just making sure you get home safely."

"As you can see, I'm home and I'm fine. I don't need a damned babysitter."

He frowned. After last night, her icy walls were back up in full force. In a matter of one night, Gauge had ruined everything that Diesel had worked so hard to get.

"Look, all I want is for us to—" Diesel's ears perked up to a faint sound above. He sniffed once and detected a familiar scent. *It's him…* He snarled and hopped out of his car, vaulting over the driver's side door without opening it. "Stay here," he told Carina. "Gauge is up there, and things are going to get a little bloody."

She blinked. "W-What?"

"I'll explain later. Just stay here." Diesel turned away from her, dropped to all fours and tore out of his clothes without a care as he shifted into his tiger form. Then he followed his brother's scent, which led him back up to the first sub-level of the parking garage. Rage took over his mind as he slowly crept along. He eyed each parked vehicle, anticipating Gauge popping out from behind one of them.

Hurried footsteps echoed behind him. Glancing back, he spotted Carina poking her head around the corner, silhouetted by a caged wall light. Something growled nearby, and Diesel returned his attention to one of the vehicles before him, a large black pickup truck. Moments later, a tiger emerged from behind it, its golden eyes glowing like two flames. Then Gauge's voice spoke in Diesel's mind, sending a shiver through his body.

"It's about time you showed up, Brother."

CHAPTER 17

Diesel swore in his mind as he slowly padded closer to the other tiger with glowing eyes staring back at him. *This can't be happening right now. Why the fuck is this happening right now?*

Letting out a low growl, Diesel projected a telepathic message to his brother, *"I don't know how you found me, asshole, but you're not leaving here alive."*

Gauge's tiger form inclined his head, keeping his gaze focused on Diesel, and began to slowly circle him. *"It took a little bit to finally find you,"* he projected in Diesel's mind.

"Did Cammy help you? Is she behind all this?"

Gauge wrinkled his nose. *"Cammy? That stupid little brat can't find her way out of bed. Why would I need* her *help?"*

Like Diesel, Gauge was also a bad liar. But as Diesel acknowledged the seriousness in Gauge's tone, he realized his brother also wasn't lying this time.

Diesel lowered his body to the ground, circling in the same direction. He was poised to strike at the slightest twitch of Gauge's muscles. *"Then what are you doing here?"* Diesel demanded.

"If by 'here,' you mean why did I leave the clan, well, the reason is the same as yours, Brother," Gauge replied.

"I wasn't kissing Axle's ass, unlike some people." Diesel sneered, baring his fangs.

"After you ran off like a scared cub, Axle's position as alpha was getting challenged frequently. The Whitetide Streak was in constant danger. Still is. Women and cubs have died at the hands of our enemies. At one point, Axle was ready to give it all up—give up everything our family had fought and died for. I was not about to let that happen, so I challenged him."

Diesel dug his claws into the concrete, thinking about his dark days in the Whitetide Streak, the only family he'd known. *"And yet, you still live... unfortunately."*

"I tried," Gauge continued. *"But at least I have the balls to admit defeat. He is strong, but he is desperate to hold on to his last bit of power."*

"Nobody has defeated him?"

"Others tried, but somehow, Axle managed to prevail. It's madness. Axle is no leader. He's unworthy to be alpha."

Diesel narrowed his eyes. *"Funny, you both said that about me."*

Gauge shook his head. *"No, Axle said it, not me. Anyway, you need to go back home and defeat that incompetent coward who has destroyed our family's honor."*

Diesel noted the desperation in his brother's tone. Things sounded serious at home, but he had moved on from that life. All that mattered anymore was him and his mate. *"That place was never home. I will not fight Axle and inherit whatever fucking war he started. I've got a new home now. A new life. And a mate."* He snarled. *"And you better keep your fucking hands off her!"*

Gauge finally stopped circling and sat, his back straight.

Diesel remained on edge and kept his body low to the ground.

"I didn't do anything to her. She had your scent all over her. I knew she was yours," Gauge projected.

"And you still *tried to take her from me?"*

"No, but making you think I did was the only way I could be certain that you were willing to fight for everything you hold dear. That you actually have the balls to stand up to anyone, no matter who they are, unlike before, when you were in the clan. You're no longer the scared little cub I remembered. You might be just the one to defeat Axle. I've been gone from home a long time, searching for a brother I wasn't sure was dead or alive."

"Well, you found me, but I will not fight. Not now, anyway. I will face him on my own terms." He wasn't sure if he would ever return to his former clan. All that waited for him there was pain. Axle had gotten his wish of being the alpha of a prominent tiger clan and the harsh responsibilities of defending it from the threats of rivals.

That was why Diesel was content with starting his own clan high in the mountains, away from the stresses of those damned clan politics.

Carina's scent suddenly filled his nose, and he glanced behind him. Her silhouette remained motionless at the corner of one of the parking garage's hulking concrete pillars.

A low growl rumbled from Gauge. *"Axle must be dealt with now. If you are willing to defend your mate, then at least defend your family's honor."*

Diesel's attention snapped back to his brother. *"I will not fight him now. And our family's honor was lost the day Aunt Evaline died."*

Gauge sneered. *"I guess I was wrong about you. You are still the weakest link of the Whitetide Streak."*

Diesel felt the fur on the back of his neck rising. *Weakest link... No, fuck them all. I'm not weak.*

"If you will not fight Axle, then you will fight me, and I will return home with news of your defeat."

A roar and a pounce sent Diesel tumbling to the ground, pinned there by his brother's great weight. His thoughts shattered, Diesel flexed his muscles and used all his strength to push up from beneath Gauge's larger body. Diesel swiped his paw at Gauge's face and made contact. Four thin, bloody lines appeared on the side of Gauge's chin. He howled and clawed back at Diesel in a barrage of swift attacks. Gauge had always been the more dexterous one, even when they'd sparred as cubs.

A claw nicked Diesel's shoulder and on the side of his neck. Blood trickled from the wounds, and a sharp, iron scent penetrated his nose.

Gauge came in with his jaws, aiming for Diesel's throat. Diesel rolled out of the way of the attack then used his body to bump Gauge off him. Gauge fell backward, his body slamming with a loud thump, and the back of his head hit the concrete. Gauge's eyes shut.

Diesel stood over his brother's body. Claws extended, Diesel buried them around Gauge's neck, drawing blood under each puncturing digit.

Gauge's eyelids fluttered open, the golden glow disappearing and revealing honey-toned eyes. Diesel flexed his muscles in show of his victory. Gauge looked up at him, opened his mouth, and the only sound that came out was a whimpering howl of pain and defeat.

A set of headlights shone on them as a car approached. Squinting, Diesel snarled and roared at the approaching vehicle, his brain rattled from the fight.

The car squealed to a halt a few meters away. Diesel's eyes adjusted to the light. He noticed a young man in the driver's seat, his face pale with fright, and Cammy riding shotgun. The passenger's door flung open, and Cammy jumped out.

"D! Wait!" she called.

Sneering, Diesel projected into his sister's mind, *"Stay the fuck away, Cam. This is* my *fight."*

Her jaw tightened. She looked behind her at her friend in the car and smacked the hood. "Thanks for the ride. Now, go. This is family business," she said to him. After a timid nod, the man put the car in reverse and squealed out of the parking garage in a blaze of white, acrid-smelling tire smoke.

Once her friend was gone, Cammy returned her attention to Diesel. She placed her index finger at the side of her temple and squeezed her eyes shut. *"D. Stop. Are you really going to kill him?"* she asked him telepathically.

For a moment, Diesel was tempted to end Gauge's life. How dare Gauge challenge him? Attempt to steal his mate? Amongst the shifter circles, that was an act of treason, punishable by death.

Gauge stared back at him with pleading, half-opened eyes. His tongue stuck out slightly. He was losing air fast.

"Killing him won't do shit," Cammy continued. *"It won't change what's going on at home. Axle will be the same asshole, still ruling as a shitty leader."*

"Gauge made mistakes. Big ones. Unforgivable ones. He has to pay," Diesel replied in her mind.

She shook her head. *"Killing him is too generous. There are other more effective ways to make him pay. Please let him go, D."*

Diesel gritted his teeth as he mulled over Cammy's words. There was some wisdom to her suggestion. Killing Gauge would only spare him his past mistakes. *Let him suffer the pains of his failures,* Diesel thought. *He's too busy worrying about the clan, so he'll never amount to anything, much less find a mate of his own.*

Damn, the Whitetide Streak was a seriously fucked-up family. No leadership, no morale, no hope. It sounded like the clan had been reduced to a bunch of weak, bewildered misfits one surprise-attack away from total annihilation. Diesel was glad he left and never looked back. There was no hope of restoring what his brothers had ultimately destroyed.

Diesel slowly released his claws from around Gauge's neck, convinced that his younger brother had conceded at last. After Diesel moved away from him, Gauge slowly rolled to his belly.

Cammy dropped her finger from her temple and let out a deep sigh. Then she opened her eyes and refocused her attention toward Diesel and Gauge.

"You... You let me live..." Gauge projected in Diesel's mind.

Diesel returned with a cool glance and lashed his tail back and forth. *"Don't make me regret my decision. Now, leave."*

Gauge lowered his head, his tail between his legs, and headed farther up the ramp toward the parking garage's main entrance. His gait had a noticeable limp. He passed by Cammy and snarled at her.

"Don't start that shit with me, Furball," Cammy spat aloud to him.

He let out an agitated roar of protest. Diesel sensed Gauge's telepathy magic as he projected a message to Cammy. Her choice of a nickname had always gotten under Gauge's skin, and Cammy knew it. Diesel found it all amusing.

"I can call you whatever the hell I want," Cammy replied aloud. "You've royally fucked up my week with your whining. You better get out of here while you still can, or *I'll* kick your ass. And I'll do it in my human form, too, just to humiliate you even more."

Gauge's attention swiveled from Cammy, then behind him to Diesel, and his eyes gave off a flash of gold. *You haven't seen the last of me, Brother. There just may be hope for this dysfunctional family yet.*

Dysfunctional. Gauge was being way too generous. Diesel gave a warning growl at him.

Gauge left the garage and slipped into the darkness of night. As soon as he was out of sight, several sharp pains struck all over Diesel's body. With his adrenaline high gone, Diesel felt every injury, bruise, and battle scar. He assumed his human form and braced himself on a concrete wall, naked and battered. Quick footsteps approached him, and Carina's and Cammy's scents overwhelmed him.

"D!"

His hand slipped away from the wall, and he collapsed into Carina's soft, yielding body. His mind was in a fog. His tiger was injured physically and scarred mentally.

Grunting, Carina struggled to support him. "D, wake up."

His eyelids fluttered. He looked at the ceiling. Carina's and Cammy's faces stared down at him from above.

"He's hurt bad. Let's take him back to your place," Cammy suggested.

Carina hesitated a moment, then nodded.

Diesel opened his mouth to protest, but his mind was too jumbled to form any coherent thought. Then, he let his eyelids flutter shut for good as he succumbed to his injuries at last.

CHAPTER 18

Diesel could still hear Carina's and Cammy's voices, long after his consciousness had slipped away. When he opened his eyes again, he found himself lying face-up on a couch in a small apartment. One sniff of the air was all he needed to realize that he was in Carina's space.

A warm and fuzzy crocheted Afghan covered his naked body. Fresh, white bandages were wrapped around his shoulders, arms, and along his collar area. His mind replayed previous events from his encounter with Gauge.

"I wish you hadn't seen all that," Cammy said from far away.

Diesel slowly turned his head. Cammy and Carina sat at a small, two-seater table in the kitchen and chatted over tea.

"What the hell did I just see happen?" Carina shrugged.

Cammy's eyelids fluttered downward, and she took a long sip from her teacup. "Long story. And not important."

"Well, I'd like to hear it." She crossed her arms. "I get ditched at dinner by a guy who ends up being yours and Gauge's *brother,* then I watch two huge tigers duke it out in the parking garage, and now I have an unconscious naked man lying on my couch. And you say it's 'not important.' *Bullshit!*"

"It's just family drama, that's all I can say."

Carina glowered. "Uh-uh. I'm not gonna be kept in the dark about this. I deserve an explanation. I'll be damned if anyone else tries to keep more secrets from me. I'm tired of the fucking secrets. I'm tired of the backstabbing."

"As much as I want to tell you, I can't, out of respect for Diesel. As he is your mate, it is his place to tell you."

Diesel continued watching them and smiled slightly, Cammy's comment easing his mind. As much as his sister pestered him, he could never deny her unwavering care and respect.

"Well, ain't like he's waking up anytime soon, so—" Carina looked over and met his gaze. Then her eyes went wide and she sprang up from her chair. "Oh! D's awake!"

Cammy followed her gaze and grinned. "So he is." She got up from the table and followed. "How ya doing, Big Brother?"

He sat upright on the couch and rubbed the side of his head. "I'll live." His gaze bounced between the two women who surrounded him.

"Are you sure you're okay?" Carina asked. "You had some nasty bruises."

"I'm fine." Diesel ripped off the bandages which were stained with his old blood. His claw wounds were healed, and his bruises disappeared. "Our kind heal fast." He handed the bandages out to Carina.

Grimacing, she looked sideways at Cammy.

"Eww…" Cammy waved her hands in front of her. "I love D, but not *that* much."

"Just this once, can you go toss them for me while I talk to him in private?" Carina emphasized with a small raise of her eyebrows.

Cammy rolled her eyes and sighed. "Ugh. You both owe me big time for this." She gingerly gathered the bandages and headed to the kitchen.

Alone, Diesel stared up silently at Carina. She returned a cool, pointed gaze, her lips pursed.

He frowned. He supposed she deserved an explanation, but he also needed her to understand that he was fighting for *her*. "I heard you two talking earlier," he began. "It is as Cammy said— just a bunch of fucked-up family drama. Gauge is trying to coerce me back to our clan in Whitetide Falls and fight my eldest brother, Axle, for the alpha position.

"Axle's been a shitty leader from what I hear, instigating fights with rival clans and other nonsense. I challenged Axle once—not long after my aunt's death—failed, and was ostracized from the clan, with a promise of death if I ever returned."

Carina scowled. "Why would your brother Gauge knowingly want to send you to your death?"

"Because he's a desperate piece of shit." Diesel growled. "And I want no part of that old life. Not anymore. Being away from that place has been the best thing I've ever done." He paused and regarded

Carina with a more intent stare. "I wouldn't have met you, otherwise…" he murmured.

A hint of pink graced her cheeks, but her displeased expression remained. "That can't be the only reason."

"It's not. I wanted my freedom. Not some obligation to fix other people's shit. I didn't want to inherit a broken clan and all its problems. The Whitetide Streak died with its last leader and most powerful alpha. Whatever is left now is a joke."

"Hasn't anyone else challenged Axle?"

"Yes, and they all failed. Funnily enough, he did not exile or kill them for it. Axle always despised me the most, and I still don't know why."

"'Cause he was jealous Aunt Evaline wanted you to be the new alpha after she was gone!" Cammy's voice called from the kitchen. "Axle only took it because he was the oldest."

Diesel rolled his eyes. "Stay out of our conversation," he said to his sister.

"This apartment's tiny and these walls are thin, so sue me."

Carina's bitter frown morphed into amusement, and she let out a light chuckle. Diesel's heart warmed, seeing her smile and laugh again.

"Anyway," he continued, "that's the short version of what's going on. I didn't want you getting caught up in it, but I guess it was gonna happen sooner or later."

Her smile disappeared again, and her face grew dark. "And what about us?"

Us... Diesel took a deep breath and let the word echo in his mind. But it was somehow distorted by the annoyed tone in her voice. "We are still bonded, forever and always since I marked you last night. Nothing will ever change that. No one will take you from me. Not even my own family. What are you worried about?"

"I've been hurt too much in my life, D. I don't want to be some flavor of the week. I know you can get any girl you want without even trying, but I'm not down for playing that game. I want to know that this 'bond' means you and me. I don't want to be with someone who plays around."

He let out a low growl. "Do you still not trust me? I fucking fought for you tonight, 'Ri. For *you.* My bond is only to you. When I say you're the only one who matters in my life, I mean it. You've got the wrong idea about me. The only woman I want is you. Fuck all your previous boyfriends who treated you like shit. I ain't one of them."

Moistening her lips, she averted her gaze and fell silent.

He reached up, wrapped his arms around her waist, and pulled her down onto his lap. The warmth of her soft ass seeped beneath the afghan that covered his nude lower half, and sprang life into his dick. "You are mine forever, and you are always worth the fight," he continued. Then he pulled her closer and planted a deep kiss on her lips. "Stay with me tonight."

She placed her hands on his chest then pulled away from the kiss. "At your place?"

"Of course."

A whistle came from the kitchen. "Wow, 'Ri! These are amazing!"

"Hm?" Carina turned her head.

Cammy bounded out of the kitchen carrying a little white book. "Oh my gosh, D! Did you see this?"

Carina gasped, her face beet-red. "Ahh! Where did you get that?"

"It was sitting on the kitchen counter next to your mail. These are so beautiful, 'Ri! You are like a goddess!"

"That's private!" Carina wriggled out of Diesel's grasp, slid off him and rushed over to Cammy.

Cammy's jaw dropped. "Are you kidding me? Private? You have *got* to show them to D!"

"No!"

"Show me what?" Diesel asked, furrowing his brow.

Carina reached for the book, but Cammy deftly swept away from her with her tiger's speed, and stood by the couch next to Diesel. "Look at your beautiful tigress-to-be!" She flipped over the book to an open spread of a photo album containing professionally-done photos of Carina dressed in green, sexy lingerie. Diesel scanned each photo, openmouthed, his mind etching every erotic pose and expression that Carina displayed. The lingerie cinched around her thick body perfectly in a way that made her extra curves smooth and flawless. She was a true model. *A tigress...*

"Stop, Cammy! Please! This is embarrassing!" Carina exclaimed, her anxious voice snapping Diesel out of his fantasy.

Smirking, Cammy closed the book and gave it back to Carina. "Okay. He's about to drool all over your couch, anyway."

"I am not drooling," Diesel protested. Then he quickly swiped the back of his hand across his mouth and glanced at it. *Still dry, thank goodness...*

Carina snatched the album, clutched it against her chest, and inclined her head. "I'm so upset right now, Cammy. I can't believe you would do that… ugh!"

"Why would you want to hide that from him?" Cammy asked. "Do you even *know* the purpose of boudoir?"

"Of course, I do! But these photos were meant for me only."

Cammy blew a raspberry. "What's the point of that? Unless you're some narcissist, or something. Well, they're your pictures, so I guess you can do whatever you want with them." She shrugged and headed for the door. "Now that D is okay, I'm heading back to the hostel to check on my roommate. He was pretty spooked tonight when he drove up and saw the raging tiger battle. He's kinda sensitive about violence, so…"

"Yeah, you do that," Carina insisted, her tone still sharp.

Cammy looked over her shoulder and waved. "See ya, Big Brother! I expect to hear some good news soon!" she piped.

What good news? he wondered, then shook his head. "Whatever. Thanks."

After Cammy left, Carina spun on her heel and toted the album down a short hallway to her bedroom. The two of them were alone in her apartment, but he no longer wanted to stay here.

Moments later, Carina stormed out of her bedroom, empty-handed, and returned to Diesel in the common room. "Sorry about all that," she muttered to him.

"Sorry about what? I should be the one who's sorry. She's my sister, after all."

"I mean, I like her and all, but she just doesn't know boundaries."

He chuckled. "Yeah. Imagine having her for a little sister. But she's harmless."

Carina chewed her bottom lip. He could smell her fear and doubt—the same stench he hated from a woman. He let out a throaty growl of displeasure. "Hey," he continued. "I really loved those photos, by the way."

She averted her gaze. "Please. Let's not talk about that."

"Why? You look beautiful. Don't you agree?"

She rubbed the back of her head. "They're just pictures."

"Why did you get them done?"

Carina glared at him. "Why? Because I wanted to. Is that a crime?"

"No. I was just… surprised, that's all."

"Surprised… or disgusted…" she muttered under her breath.

His keen tiger hearing picked up her comment, and he raised his eyebrows. "Disgusted? Are you kidding me? I want to see you in that lingerie again. You are fucking hot."

She opened her mouth then closed it again.

"Do you still not believe that I'm into you? After the way I claimed you?"

She avoided his gaze again and didn't respond.

"Maybe I just need to show you again. Maybe you weren't paying attention before. Maybe I should make you cum five times this time instead of four."

A hint of a smile tugged at her lips, and she slowly looked back at him.

"So, you're going to stay with me tonight, right?" Diesel continued.

She paused a beat, thinking for a moment, then gave him a slight nod. "Okay. But what about you? We couldn't salvage your clothes after they were ripped to shreds from your shifting, and I don't have anything in my closet that would fit you."

Diesel stood from the couch and secured the afghan around his waist like a towel. "There."

Carina scanned him up and down, then burst out laughing.

That beautiful smile again. Diesel intended to make her smile all night tonight.

CHAPTER 19

THE MORE DIESEL THOUGHT ABOUT the encounter in the parking garage, the more he regretted letting this brother go free. There was no hope for Gauge taking over the Whitetide Streak if he was going to pull such stupid shit. After all those years of mocking Diesel for backing out of the imminent war that Axle was starting with the other clans, both of his brothers ended up being the real cowards. Gauge was better off dead than trying to redeem himself, much less surviving in the city. There wasn't a woman on the planet who would take him seriously.

Diesel wanted to think that there was something else up with his brother. Gauge had been hunting him down for a long time, but it couldn't have been just because he wanted to give Diesel a message from home. Like Diesel, Gauge was reserved when he wanted to be. If he had dark secrets, he would make sure no one ever knew.

A cool draft whisked between Diesel's legs under the crocheted afghan tied around his waist. He shivered, his mind returning to the present. His bare foot slipped briefly off the accelerator as he squeezed his thighs together to prevent the uncomfortable draft.

His phone screen lit up in the console with a silent incoming call. It was Leah. Frowning, he ignored it and turned back to the road.

"Aren't you gonna answer that?"

Diesel looked sideways at Carina in the passenger seat. She glared back at him.

"Nope," Diesel replied, returning his attention to the road.

"Who's Leah?"

"Just a friend."

"Look, if you want to talk to her, then talk to her. I'm not some jealous bitch."

Diesel gritted his teeth, her comment roiling his blood. "I never said or thought you were, nor would I ever. I don't want to talk to her, possibly ever, after the way she royally fucked me over and humiliated me in front of her friends. Friends don't do that to each other."

Carina paused. "Wait, was she one of the women from that baby shower?"

He bared his fangs in disgust. "She was the Hen Queen, yeah…"

Carina suddenly burst out laughing.

Diesel snarled. "What the hell are *you* laughing at?"

She wiped away a stray tear. "Are you still salty about that baby shower?"

He growled. "Yes, and I don't think it's very funny."

"I'm sorry. Just the thought of a grumpy guy like you waltzing around in a room full of balloons and teddy bears is hilarious."

"I'm not grumpy."

"You are. Sometimes you just need to laugh off the stupid shit that happens in life. There's no sense in being upset over it. There are far better things to do with your time." She paused and grinned cheekily. "I guess I should take my own advice, too, eh?"

Diesel considered her words and smiled slightly. She was right, of course. He'd let Leah's antics get to him for too long. And he did have much better things to do—like taking Carina home and claiming her in his bed.

"And if it makes you feel better," Carina continued, "I don't like baby showers, either. I get envious of the mother-to-be. It's a constant reminder of my desire for a family."

"You and I aren't that much different."

Carina smiled and propped her elbow on the rolled-down passenger's window. She stared out the window then muttered, "Damn, tonight has got to be some sort of weird-ass dream."

"Nightmare is more like it," Diesel said.

"All I wanted was a nice, quiet, enjoyable dinner and no games. Instead, I get ditched then witness a tiger fight, and now I'm being driven around by a half-naked man wearing a granny afghan as a damn loincloth!"

He laughed. "But this half-naked man's gonna take you home and give you a night to remember."

Crossing her arms, she blew a raspberry. "I still haven't forgotten the other night."

"Damn right."

"That's not funny. I'm still sore." She pouted.

"That's what you get for thinking wolves are sexier than tigers."

She rolled her eyes. "My bad."

He sneered, a low growl rumbling in his throat. "And I can't believe that you would even consider going to dinner with Gauge."

"It wasn't anything serious. Before that night you claimed me, I didn't know what would happen between us. And when Gauge told me all those horrible things about you, I let my emotions take over. It felt like déjà vu, you know?"

He scowled. "He intended to turn you against me. To rile me up to fight."

"I don't get it. If Axle is hated so much, why do people still follow him?"

"Because his followers are weak-minded and easily swayed by his bullshit."

"That sounds like a real mess." She reached her hand behind her neck then chewed her bottom lip. "What does our bond mean, if you have no clan?"

His throat tightened at her question, and he carefully considered his words. Freedom from his broken family never felt so good. And having Carina as his mate made it even better. "I may be ostracized from my former clan, but that doesn't mean I can't start my own. I'm still a Whitetide tiger by blood."

Carina blinked. "Your *own* clan? Sounds like it will be a difficult undertaking."

"It will be, at first. I will have to prove myself worthy of the alpha title to other clans who may try and invade my space. But this time, I will be ready. I will show my brothers what a *real* alpha looks like."

Diesel pulled up to the cabin a short while later. They got out of the car, and Diesel escorted Carina inside. He shut the door, leaned his back against it, and exhaled a huge sigh. It was good to finally be home.

"Now the fun begins," he said, eyeing her mischievously.

Her eyebrows rose. "Excuse me, but you're still wearing my afghan."

He unwrapped it from his waist and tossed it over the back of the couch. He returned to her and caught her gaze focused downward. He smirked. "Better?"

Her gaze quickly turned upward, and she cleared her throat. "I, uh..."

Smiling, he took her hand and led her to the master suite. "Come. Let's get cleaned up."

She walked with him, not resisting his lead. "I shouldn't stay for too long. I have to work tomorrow."

"Call in sick."

Carina let out a hollow laugh. "I wish. I've got bills."

"Now that you're my mate, you don't have to trouble yourself working at a job you hate."

"And how do you figure that?"

He stopped in the doorway of the master bathroom. "Thanks to the success of my gym and my various other business investments, you can consider yourself financially secure."

"That's sweet of you, D, but if I'm going to live with you, I want to do my fair share."

"You can always work with me at the gym."

She chewed her bottom lip. "Don't make jokes, D…"

"I'm serious. In *my* gym, everyone has their own goals. I've employed all types of trainers of various backgrounds and specialties."

"And what exactly is my specialty?"

He winked. "You have one hell of a roundhouse kick. I can definitely see you leading a women's cardio-kickboxing class. What do you think?"

Carina fought down a smile. "I think you're crazy, but it sounds like it could be fun. Sure beats flipping burgers all day and coming home smelling like french fry grease."

He chuckled. "Damn right. And as my mate, you will also rule beside me as we create a strong, resilient clan—much stronger than the former Whitetide could ever be. Your duties will be to the clan, as will mine."

She bit her bottom lip. "What sort of duties?"

"Like protecting these lands from intruders. Training our future family to fight…" He smirked. "You think all that stuff we did at the gym was just to help you lose weight? Hell fucking no. I love you the way you are."

She blinked several times. "So you *were* tricking me into staying at your gym so I could keep paying you?"

"It wasn't a trick. I was teaching you fighting basics. Because I had hoped one day you would be mine. And I want a strong tigress who will always protect her home and her family. Now, enough talking. I want to enjoy you tonight."

Carina's breath hitched when she peered into the bathroom. Right then, he realized he hadn't shown her this part of the cabin. The finished-wood tub added to the rustic charm of the bathroom—just how he liked it. His cabin was cozy but always reminded him of the outdoors. He didn't feel like a bath, though. The matching finished-wood shower looked more appealing.

"I've never seen a wood tub or shower before," Carina said, running her hand along the finish.

He let go of her hand. "Sounds like I need to give you a firsthand experience, then." Smirking, he slowly lowered the straps of her dress.

She watched his hand briefly then helped him along. He moved behind her and unzipped the back of her dress. He peeled the dress away from her luscious, curvy body then took a moment to admire her form, bringing life into his dick. It stood fully erect and stiff, throbbing with need. *Damn,* the effect this woman had on him!

Carina giggled, wriggling out of her bra and panties. "Someone's excited."

You have no idea. He licked his lips greedily, eager to suck on those dark nipples and have another taste between those legs. His brain was in a fog, and he couldn't respond, so he turned on the shower spray. His mind wandered again to the other night. And he knew exactly how he could make the night even better.

"Showering with a hot guy. Damn, it's been a secret fantasy," Carina said.

His eyes widened, and his dick pulsed. "Wait. You've *never* showered with a guy before?"

She shook her head, her cheeks reddening. "Guys were too disgusted to see me naked, much less want me to take a shower with them."

"Their loss." He opened the glass shower door and pulled her inside.

He pressed his lips to hers as the warm spray rained down on their bodies. Leaning against the wall, he pulled her into him. Her ass pressed against his hard dick while the water peppered her front. He brushed his hands down her smooth arms and chest then across her waist, exploring every soft curve of her body. She moaned softly.

He lathered his hands with a bar of soap and slowly trailed his hands between her legs. His fingers grazed her clit, and she flinched, but he held her still, flicking her folds with careful precision. Her body shuddered, and her forbidden pearl hardened beneath the pads of his fingers. He slipped a finger inside her, and she gasped, groping backward to use him for stability. He kissed along her neck and across her shoulder as he guided his soapy finger in and out of her with ease. After a final thrust, he withdrew his finger and continued exploring the rest of her body.

He ran his hands over her soft, voluptuous ass, making it slick and soapy. He squeezed her cheeks greedily then gave one a gentle, playful slap.

She squealed and flinched, her movements causing her ass to jiggle even more.

Tantalized by her body's movements, he felt a surge of pain through his dick. "Damn, you have such a perfect ass," he whispered in her ear.

She nibbled on her bottom lip nervously.

He guided the shower spray to rinse off her front. While the water relentlessly pelted her skin, he slid into her pussy from behind.

"Ahh! D!" she cried, her walls eagerly clamping on their throbbing intruder. He thrust into her hard and furious, his dick thirsting for her core. He relished the feel of her soapy ass against him. His hands found their way to her stiff nipples. He flicked them with his thumbs then tugged with his fingers. He cupped her breasts and squeezed them, noting their firmness. She cried out in pain, and he grinned knowingly. *Still sensitive there.*

He thrust his hips into her, faster, stronger. The feel of her curves drew out his tiger. She moaned louder, bracing herself against the wall as he pressed deeper into her, eventually reaching her core. Her walls constricted his dick mercilessly.

"Fuck..." he growled, triggering his feral beast. He reached down to grope a handful of her belly fat and was done for. Her softness, her scent, and her body's reactions were like an emotional high. It surged through his body and out his dick, filling her with everything he had. He came so hard and so much that some of his seed leaked out of her and pooled onto the shower floor before the water sent it away in a swirl of white.

She felt so warm inside that he wanted to stay in her, but he needed to wash himself before the two of them turned to prunes. He pulled out of her and moved her out of the shower spray. As she braced herself against the wall, her eyelids fluttered, and she looked at him, seemingly in a daze.

He turned away and soaped up his own body. As soon as he finished rinsing off, he felt two hands on his back. He froze then turned his head, looking behind him. It was Carina's turn to explore him. She guided her lathered hands across his back and down to his ass.

Damn, her hands feel good there.

"Turn around," she said.

His smile grew. He turned off the shower and faced her.

Her lips crashed into his in a deep, passionate kiss. She pulled back and looked at him, her lids heavy. "I'm falling for you hard, D..."

He licked his lips, tasting the remnants of her, and exhaled. "I've already fallen for you, 'Ri."

"Fuck me again. Hard. Raw. Please."

He growled in delight. She didn't need to ask twice. He lifted one of her legs slightly and slid back into her. With her back pressed against the shower wall, she had nowhere to go. He pinned her there with his weight as he pounded into her.

"You're mine," he growled in a voice not quite his own. His tiger was fighting to tear through, but he concentrated hard to keep it at bay. "You're... all... mine..."

"I'm yours, D. I'll be your mate. I'll bear your children. I'll lead this clan beside you."

Their bodies moved in a fast, steady rhythm. Carina moaned as he pumped her hard and deep. The smacking sound of her pussy was an erotic symphony to his keen tiger ears. With a grunt, Diesel drove his dick to her breaking point and settled there a moment, letting his member throb against her cervix.

"Mmm… right… there…" he muttered.

"D… ohhh… I feel it… so much…" she whined. "Fill me… please…"

He closed his eyes. His dick swelled, and he gave another hard thrust. It was truly the most beautiful words he'd heard her utter.

They moaned and breathed in unison as they reached their peak. She was the first to break. The warmth of her orgasm spread over his dick, and he responded with another hard wave of cum that filled her until it was bloated and tight with his hot seed. The ordeal left him physically exhausted.

Out of breath, they finally left the shower, toweled off, and cuddled in his king-sized bed. With his arms wrapped around Carina's warm, naked body, he listened to her steady heartbeat as she drifted off to sleep. Carina had declared herself his, and their bond sealed that promise. His heart swelled. This was truly the happiest day of his life.

CHAPTER 20

One week later...

Diesel pulled up along the curb at the entrance to the train station and put his car in park. He leaned his head against the seat's headrest and sighed. Finally, after a crazy two-week adventure, his time with his little sister had come to an end. But for how long? he wondered.

Cammy stared straight ahead at the narrow street that was bathed in an orange hue by the setting sun. The deep frown on her face told a curious story. Would she be back? Or was she so genuinely mortified about Gauge's sudden appearance that she would travel far, far away?

Not looking at her, Diesel broke the monotonous silence. "You got everything?"

Cammy puffed her cheeks.

Diesel swiveled his gaze to her, then lifted an eyebrow. "What's wrong now? Don't tell me you're having second thoughts about leaving."

She slowly turned her head to him. "You didn't tell me you were going to start your own clan."

"You didn't ask."

"I had to hear it secondhand from Carina. You realize Axle isn't going to like that too much, right?"

"I don't give a fuck. I dare him to come find and challenge me. I don't know why you're so upset about it, anyway."

She quirked a smile. "Who said I was upset? I think it's brilliant, actually. Somebody needs to humble him, because that furball, Gauge, sure ain't gonna do it."

His mind returned to his younger brother for a moment. The way he'd slinked off into the darkness that night, defeated, Diesel sensed he would probably not see him again. But he still questioned the real purpose of Gauge's visit. If it really was to employ Diesel's help, or was it something else. After a week of not seeing Gauge since that night they battled, Diesel wondered about the latter.

"I just want to live in peace with my family," Diesel said at last. "No drama, no stress."

"Well," Cammy said. "If you really are starting this new clan, then I get to be in it, too."

Diesel rolled his eyes. "Did you not hear what I just said? I want to live in peace."

"So do I. So does everyone. C'mon, D. At least let me be the omega."

Diesel grimaced at her suggestion of such a lowly position. "Why the hell do you want to be the omega?"

"Um, hello? Zero responsibilities, and never having to worry about being pressured into finding a mate? Fuck yes, sign me up, damn it."

Diesel fought down a smile. Her amusing, trickster qualities certainly made her an ideal candidate for the position. "What makes you think I even want you in my clan?" he said.

"You can't bullshit me, D. You know I'm your favorite."

He blew a raspberry. "Favorite pain in the ass?"

She laughed. "You're as predictable as a bad joke."

"I'll think about it."

Smirking, Cammy grabbed her duffel bag and opened the passenger door. "See you soon."

Diesel left their conversation at that and watched her head into the train station, onward to whatever new adventure awaited her. Afterward, he drove off.

A ride through the city on a Sunday evening was what he needed to get his mind off his whirlwind of emotions. His mate and new clan were his priority now. He'd planned to fix up and secure his cabin and prepare it for the growth of his new family.

Diesel's attention shifted to the familiar apartment buildings and businesses along the main street he drove. It wasn't until two days ago that Carina had finally told Diesel where Gauge had been working. On one hand, Diesel was furious that she'd withheld that information for so long, but she was worried about Diesel doing something stupid. Not that he would, but the fact that Gauge was somewhere in the same city as him felt more like a threat to Diesel's space.

Diesel's curious tiger mulled over the possibility of discovering his brother there—if Gauge was still foolish enough to stay.

He located the address of the auto shop on his phone and followed it to the destination on the map. Minutes later, he was sitting outside a nondescript brick building with an attached two-bay garage. A big white banner hanging above the shop's main office read "Under New Management." Shadowy movement slinked about inside one of the bays. Diesel clenched his jaw. *That fucking bastard has the balls to still be here?*

Diesel got out of his car and marched straight into the open bay where the mysterious stranger paced about. The stranger was a hefty man who walked with a solid gait—too solid to be Gauge. A dirt-smeared towel draped over his shoulder and a torque wrench in his hand, the man approached a car that was secured on a lift. He wore a blue work shirt with a white oval name patch that read 'Barron.' Whistling a lighthearted tune, he adjusted one of the front wheel hub bearings and then began securing a lugnut around the assembly.

Diesel cleared his throat. Barron stopped whistling and looked his way.

"Yeah? What can I do for you?" Barron asked, his voice low and gruff.

Diesel looked left and right, then sniffed the air. Gauge's scent was nowhere to be found. Then again, it could've been masked by the various grimy scents of the auto shop. "Where's Gauge?"

Barron arched a thick eyebrow. "Who wants to know?"

"His brother—Diesel."

Barron's other eyebrow arched. "Oh yeah? Well I ain't his keeper." He chuckled to himself and resumed securing the rest of the assembly.

Diesel let out a low growl. "Listen, smartass. I gave him a warning to get the fuck out of this city. If he's still here…"

"Look, I don't give two shits about your family drama. I don't know where he is."

"This is his shop, isn't it?"

"Was. It's under new management now—me."

Diesel opened his mouth, then retracted his reply by wrinkling his nose. "Wait… what?"

"He don't work here no more," Barron continued. "Last week, he told me he was going away. Didn't say where."

"You didn't ask?"

"I did, but he said it was none of my business, so I left it at that. Whatever. I ain't one to stick my nose where it don't belong. Before Gauge left, he signed the business over to me, and here I am. So, like I said before, I don't know where your brother is."

Diesel rubbed the back of his head, feeling both confused and shocked. Just like that, Gauge really is gone...

CHAPTER 21

Four months later...

CARINA ROLLED OFF HER AIR mattress that morning, half-awake and half-stuck in another amazing dream about Diesel that made her pussy ache. Hell, her pussy hadn't stopped aching since the first signs of her pregnancy. Just the sight of her small baby bump kept him horny. And the bigger it grew, the more intense he got.

Carina was smitten. She still hadn't gotten used to being a shifter's mate, and pregnancy was a whole new world for her. Having tiger-shifter children growing inside of her did all sorts of things to her body, altering it in a way that reformed her human biological makeup to be touched by the threads of magic. In less than a month, she was going to be a mother. She wondered how many children she would be having. She and Diesel had decided to keep that a surprise.

The day she'd learned about her pregnancy was the last day she'd consulted with her boudoir album. Her dreams of having a family of her own had erased the sadness and doubt from her mind. And having Diesel for a mate was the greatest gift she cherished.

She trudged out of her room, which was empty after the last of her possessions had been either sold or donated the day before. She'd lived in the same apartment since graduating high school. This apartment had memories, both good and bad, and today, she carried out the final day of her lease. Even after declaring her devotion to Diesel as his mate, she'd remained at her apartment until the very end to give herself closure on her old life. Of course, Diesel didn't take too kindly to that decision.

Carina entered the bathroom and stared at her unkempt reflection in the mirror. She no longer saw the old self-conscious Carina who lived a boring life. Instead, she saw a leader. A *tigress*. Someone who was loved and adored by the most amazing man she'd ever met. Her devotion to her new life had given her the courage to quit her job at Dice 'n Grill three weeks ago.

Her cell phone suddenly rang in the bedroom. It was most likely Diesel checking up on her again. Since she'd first found out she was pregnant, he called her endlessly whenever they were apart. It'd been sweet at first, but it had become downright annoying. Carina understood his concern, however, especially when she'd decided to live in her apartment for the remainder of her lease rather than move in with him right away.

"Good morning, my sexy tigress," Diesel said in a loving tone. "How are you feeling?"

"Like a ton of bricks." Carina laughed.

"Do you need help? Should I come over?" His voice carried deep concern.

"No, D. I'm fine, really. A buyer came over yesterday afternoon and trucked off the last of the furniture and things from the apartment. I made over seven grand from everything. I never realized the amount of shit I'd accumulated over the years in here."

"It does add up quickly," Diesel said. "I'm glad to hear you finally sold everything, but I wish you'd just leave that damn apartment already."

She gave a light chuckle. "Well, you'll be happy to know that, as of today, my lease is up and I'll be turning in the keys."

He gasped. "Seriously? Holy shit, that's the best news I've heard since you got pregnant."

She bit her bottom lip, remembering the night she'd told him the news. She'd gotten him so turned on she'd ended up with a sore, exhausted pussy after fucking him all night and well into the next morning.

"So that means you have nothing else holding you there," Diesel continued. "So say your final goodbyes and get your pretty ass down to this gym before I come carry you away caveman-style."

She wasn't opposed to that at all, but she knew he would have her working a sweat first before he'd let her have any fun. "I was hoping I could finally get some practice with teaching a cardio-kickboxing class."

"And risk going into early labor in the middle of my gym? Hell no. If you're going to go into early labor, it'll be while I'm fucking you in my bed."

Carina rolled her eyes. "For our sake, I hope I do not go into early labor at all."

"Look, there will be plenty of time afterward to teach class. Right now, I'm just worried about you."

"That's sweet of you, D, but I'll be fine. So what kind of workout are you going to have me do this time?"

"You'll see. Now that you're officially all mine, I have the perfect workout in mind."

She could hear the mischief in his voice, and Carina knew her pussy was going to start aching again once he was done.

After she said her final goodbyes to some of her neighbors and handed the keys to her landlord, Carina took the bus downtown. Her old hatchback had finally bitten the dust last month, and she hadn't bothered investing in another car. The bus stopped at the light where Gauge's auto shop sat on the corner. She glanced out the tinted window at one of the open-bay work areas. A small part of her wondered if he had ever returned. She hadn't seen or heard from Gauge since that night he and Diesel fought in the parking garage.

As the bus drove off again, so did Carina's thoughts shift away from Gauge and to Cammy.

Her whereabouts were unknown, but Diesel warned Carina that she would probably be back. Cammy's mannerisms were more direct and forward than what Carina was used to, but in the end, Carina was grateful for her nudges. There was a lot she wanted to thank Cammy for, and she'd hoped that she would return at some point to see her new niece or nephew.

For now, however, Cammy was gone, just like Gauge, and all Carina could do was wonder.

Diesel punched a hanging bag repeatedly, sending every bit of his anger and frustration into the canvas. Sweat dripped from his forehead as he maintained his intense training. He had to get stronger—for not only himself, but his new clan, as well. Soon, he would have to face Axle, and he would be ready. He hadn't seen Gauge in months and wondered if he'd gone off to train, too. Fighting his brothers was the last thing he wanted, but the day he struck out on his own, Diesel had known the battle was inevitable. Soon, he would have a family of his own and a beautiful mate to rule beside him.

"Hey, boss, got the final papers signed. Looks like everything's good to go."

Diesel stopped and looked over his shoulder at Rick, his second-in-command. Rick had been a part of the Nine Stars Gym since its inception, and Diesel knew he would be leaving things in capable hands as he began his new life with Carina. "Good. Then why the hell are you calling me 'boss'?" He grinned.

Rick smiled and gave a mock salute. "I won't let you down, man."

"I know you won't." After Rick left, Diesel took off his boxing gloves and stuffed them into his duffel bag. A small wooden box poked out from under a shirt. He swiped the box and stared at it. He'd been stalling to give it to Carina, and he didn't know why. There was no better opportunity than now. He ran his fingers over the box's smooth finish. It had been sitting in the bottom of his bag for way too long.

He slipped the box in his pocket and shouldered his bag. As he headed toward the showers, light from the front entrance caught his eye. Carina walked in, wearing a lime-green workout tank, which stretched across her enormous belly, and grey yoga pants. His dick throbbed at the sight. She waddled through the gym while she rubbed her sexy belly. Being pregnant certainly amplified her beauty.

Diesel's bag slid to the floor with a thump. The sight of her riled his senses, urging his tiger to break free.

"So what's this special workout you have in mind?" Carina asked with a smirk.

He shook himself out of his thoughts then focused on her face. "Oh, the workout isn't here, dear. We need to go someplace more... comfortable." He leaned in to kiss her cheek then moved to her mouth. He caressed the side of her face as his eyes drank up the rest of her body. Her pregnancy had made her breasts fuller and heavier, and he was continuously drawn to them. Her hips and ass were rounder and softer, with even more curves to grab for his pleasure. She'd gained back the pounds she'd lost while training, but she no longer seemed self-conscious about her body. Carina was a curvy, thick girl, and she still wore the weight well.

Her eyebrows shot up. "And where did you have in mind?"

He gave her another quick kiss on the lips then took her left hand in his. "You'll see. But first..."

He pulled the box from his pocket and flipped it open. A small wooden ring carved with intricate tribal symbols and trimmed in polished tiger's eye stone was nestled snugly in the box's velvet insert.

Her eyes widened, and her jaw dropped. She sucked in a breath and squeezed his hand. "H-Holy shit..." she whispered.

Smiling warmly, he took out the ring. "Our bond was sealed the night I marked you as mine, but I want to seal that bond even further. You will lead and fight beside me and be the most amazing mother to our children. This ring once belonged to my aunt. She gave it to me when I was younger, in hopes that I would become alpha of the Whitetide Streak. But things didn't go as planned. I let her down, but I kept the ring, promising myself that it would belong to my future mate." He slipped the ring on her finger and kissed it. "This rightfully belongs to you, Carina. You are mine forever."

Carina admired the ring, and her eyes became glassy. Her bottom lip quivered. "This... This is... the greatest day of my life," she said in a choked voice.

His smile grew. "Every day I spend my life with you is a great day." He joined his lips with hers, and his hand fell over her taut belly, rubbing it gently.

"Score, Diesel!" someone yelled.

Diesel and Carina broke their kiss in time to see the small crowd gathered around them. They were suddenly met with cheers and whistles from the gym staff.

Rick gave Diesel a thumbs-up. "You two lovebirds get outta here, eh? We got this."

Smiling, Diesel picked up his duffel bag and wrapped his arm around Carina's waist. "Yeah. Good idea. See you fools later." He gave his coworkers a mock salute then escorted Carina to the exit.

Diesel didn't think the evening could get any better. But when Carina surprised him with the most delicious steak-and-potatoes dinner he'd ever had, he was in absolute bliss. His belly full, he stared across the table at his beautiful mate and smiled. She'd spoiled him, and he vowed to repay the gesture later in his bedroom.

Carina got up slowly then began clearing the table.

Diesel sprang up and snatched the dishes from her. "Gimme those," he said, toting them to the sink. He left them there for now, promising to clean them later.

She fought down her smile as she rolled her eyes. "For fuck's sake, D. It's no big deal. I'm more than capable of doing that."

He returned to her and kissed her lips. "I know, but I need you to save that energy."

"What?"

He picked her up and carried her in his arms with ease. All that heavyweight training he'd done for months had finally paid off. She was heavy, but she was still perfect.

She squealed. "Ah! What are you doing?"

Grinning, he carried her off to the master bedroom. "We had our dinner. Now it's time for dessert."

"Oooh..."

He carefully lay her in bed and hovered over her on all fours, then ravished her lips. She moaned against his lips and rubbed her fingers against the shadow of a beard along his cheek. He let out a low growl in his throat and deepened the kiss. Slowly, he guided his kisses downward. He helped her out of the tank top and tossed it to the floor, his own shirt off and gone in seconds.

His gaze zeroed in on her firm breasts currently trapped in the confines of her sports bra. The outlines of her large nipples protruded from beneath the stretchy fabric. Smirking, he teased her nipples with the pads of his thumbs.

"Ah..." She flinched.

Her breasts were even more sensitive lately, and he loved it. No doubt, he could make her cum with his insistent teasing. He finally pulled off the bra and tossed it in the growing pile of discarded clothing. Piece by piece, the rest of their clothes were peeled off until he was skin to skin with her.

He cupped her breasts and kneaded them gently. He ran his tongue across her hardened nipples then sucked on each of them greedily.

She hissed. "Ugh! That hurts. D-Don't suck... Please..." She dug her fingers through his hair, her nails scratching his scalp.

He moaned, the sharp pains she inflicted driving his libido. Her torture was his pleasure. He pressed down on her erect nipple with his tongue, then covered it with his needy mouth again. Shutting his eyes, he sucked her, slow and steady.

She cried out, her body shuddering. The fresh scent of her orgasm filled his nose.

He released her nipple from his mouth with a wet pop. "Did you just cum already?" He gazed at her with hooded eyes.

She swallowed. A small hint of red flushed her cheeks. "I can't help that they are so sensitive," she whispered.

Small white beads appeared at the tip of her nipples, then slowly trickled down her breasts. "Full of your delicious milk," he whispered, then lapped up the white streams with his tongue.

"Don't get greedy," she murmured.

He let out a small chuckle, reining in his curious tiger from indulging. "Good thing for you, I can't taste sweet things."

"Even if you did, the cubs need it much more."

"I know." He smirked. They were going to have a fun night. He ran his hand down over her taut belly. His dick throbbed at the thought of his dream of having his own family coming true. He never thought being in such a position could feel so powerful. The desire to protect everything about this woman was beyond anything he could have imagined.

Fuck... is this... love?

"Shit," she hissed. "Your hands feel so good."

And he loved having his hands—and his mouth—on her. He slid down the length of her body, kissing her, tasting the sheen of sweat from her skin. He kissed all over her huge belly while, gentle and urging, his hands skillfully massaged her.

He kneaded her soft, fleshy sides while he kissed her belly button. She squirmed and moaned in protest, and the strong musk of her arousal flooded his senses.

"You came again," he said, not breaking his insistent kisses down the forbidden line of her belly.

Her breathing became ragged as he drew closer to her center. More hot juices pooled on the bedding beneath her.

"What a waste of a good dessert," he murmured, parting her legs. "I'll just have to make you cum again so I can have my fill."

She whimpered something incoherent in response.

He ran his tongue along her inner thigh, tasting remnants of her nectar. A delicious tease, but he intended to have more. His tongue made its way to her clit, starting with a gentle flick then swirling around every pink petal. His eyelids fluttered as he relished her wonderfully addicting taste. He felt her squirm, but he held her still with his strength. He would torture her mind and body until she could no longer take it.

His tongue slid up and down the slick folds of her clit then slid inside her. Her extreme tightness from the pregnancy gave him a buzz.

"Oh, fuck! D!" she cried out. Unable to move, her body shivered beneath his touch, her hands white-knuckling the bedding.

He skillfully swirled his tongue along her tight, clamping walls, urging her body to let go. Withdrawing his tongue, he sucked her clit again, harder, sensing it was more sensitive than her breasts. He needed to taste all of her. His hands ran along her thighs, groping her skin, then traveled up to her belly, where his gentle massage continued.

She wailed, and her body convulsed. She finally reached her breaking point, and the hot rush of her orgasm filled his waiting mouth.

The sound of her cries and the taste of her nectar caused a small spurt of pre-cum to escape his control. A low growl rumbled in his throat as he felt his tiger tearing through his subconscious.

Yes... Fuck yes. So delicious... his tiger praised in his mind as he indulged in every last drop.

He rose from her, licking her succulent juice from his lips. She breathed heavily and looked back at him with half-opened eyes.

"D..." she whispered.

He shook his head. "Your workout's not over yet, tigress."

Her mouth opened slightly. "W-What?"

He grinned and slid off her. He lay behind her in bed, wrapped his arms around her, and pulled her to him until her ass pressed against his dick. He kissed her upper back and over the scar of her mark as he slowly ground his hips against her ass.

"Wait," she croaked.

He halted. "What's wrong?"

She sighed. "Be gentle..."

Kissing her mark, he caressed her belly with his hand. "Of course, I will—until you give me a reason not to."

She exhaled slowly, her body relaxing to his touch.

He moved her leg with his, giving him access to her dripping-wet pussy. He pushed into her tightness, being gentle yet firm, and hissed. "Damn, girl, you're tight as fuck," he grunted.

She moaned with each insistent thrust. Her walls clamped his steel dick once he was far enough inside. His breathing faltered. His hand found its way up to one of her breasts and groped hard, then flicked and fondled her erect nipple with his thumb.

He moved his hips in a slow, steady rhythm, and she matched his pace. He drew in and out of her, working up his orgasm hard and fast. She increased the speed, and he joined her, their harried breaths synching.

"Fuck me, D! Fuck me hard, D!" she chanted breathily.

Her demands triggered his tiger. He exhaled, and the colors in his vision muted. Fuck, he needed to release before he ended up doing something out of his control.

He clenched his teeth and said in a gruff voice, "My... tigress... I love you..."

He splayed both hands across her belly and slammed into her. She cried out, open-mouthed, and her body shuddered.

"Tell me you want more," he moaned between breaths.

"Y...Yes... m... more," she croaked.

He ground her in a steady, rhythmic motion, grunting and groaning as he kept his tiger at bay for as long as he could. He gave her a final thrust then released in her with a satisfied groan. Amid his own scent, he caught hers, too, as strong and delectable as ever.

A strange sensation rippled under his hands as they rode the height of their orgasm. He perked up, his tiger on alert.

"The baby moved," she whispered, easing his concern.

Smiling like a proud father-to-be, he kissed her scar on her back again.

They collapsed with an exhausted breath and remained cuddled in a spooning position with him still inside her. Diesel closed his eyes, relishing the warmth of his dick nestled inside her pussy, the feel of her soft body against his, and the tightness of her belly beneath his hand. He kissed and tenderly licked the mark on the back of her neck. *Mine.*

The rippling sensations in her belly continued. Diesel grinned. "That one must be a fighter."

Carina let out an airy chuckle. Then she placed her hand over his on her belly. "D..."

"What is it, my tigress?" he asked, not opening his eyes.

"I love you."

EPILOGUE

Two months later...

CAMMY STEPPED OUTSIDE THE CABIN and inhaled the fresh, crisp, mountain air. The soft grass beneath her paws was coated with morning dew. It was a perfect fall morning for a walk through the woods—or in Diesel's terms, 'patrolling.' So much for having no responsibilities.

Being an omega had more benefits than drawbacks for Cammy. Diesel's clan was still dangerously small, but over time, that would change. For now, however, he was happy just being a family man, and Cammy was happy being the cool aunt to two beautiful little cubs—a boy and girl—Zahair and Indira.

Carina and Diesel were so selfishly in love with each other, it was maddening. And Cammy adored the madness. It gave her a reason to tease Diesel even more. It wasn't long before Carina was knocked up again. Despite her pregnancy, she still worked alongside Diesel at home, and at his gym.

The endless forest stretched well beyond the forty acres of Diesel's secured territory. Since the clan's new formation, his territory had only been contested once by outsiders, which ended up being a small herd of deer shifters—hardly a threat. But after Diesel had made his presence known, all had been quiet ever since. The idea of patrolling seemed like overkill to Cammy, but she only went along with it because she was bored out of her mind, being left home alone on babysitting duty.

With the cubs still asleep so early in the morning, Cammy took the opportunity to get some work done, as well as enjoy a little dip in the lake. She maintained an empathic link with the cubs, who were safely inside the locked cabin. At the slightest feeling of discomfort from either of them, Cammy would know.

At last, she reached the dock at the bank of Lake Hyacinth. The morning light danced off the water's surface. Birds tweeted happily, and the morning insects accompanied the ambient, serene song of nature.

No wonder D loves living here. Total opposite from the old home. Cammy stood at the edge of the dock. Her tail lashed about as she gazed at the water, watching the tiny minnows swimming beneath, and dragonflies hovering just above its surface.

After taking another moment to concentrate on her empathic link with her niece and nephew—still snoozing—Cammy dove into the water. The cool, refreshing sensation over her fur brought memories of her childhood, when she and her siblings would swim all day every day in beautiful Lake Greyson back at their old home. She floated on her back and closed her eyes, savoring those pleasant memories that she wished she'd see again. But times changed, and so did her brothers, unfortunately, for the worst.

A faint sound of a tree branch snapping nearby suddenly piqued her senses. Cammy opened her eyes and stared up at the morning sky. She rolled back over and paddled in place, scanning the area.

She was almost in the middle of the large lake, but the dock wasn't far away.

Another tree branch snapped, and Cammy perked her ears. She sniffed the air. Nothing discernable other than bass, perch, and rainbow trout. Still, her curious tiger was intrigued. She quickly swam back. As she reached the shore, she scanned the tree-lined area again and listened. The mysterious sounds were gone, replaced by the serene sounds of nature. Again, she smelled nothing out of the ordinary but the lake and its surrounding vegetation.

Ugh, I'm becoming Diesel, getting all paranoid over nothing. She shook off the excess water from her fur, then licked her scraggly mess of a coat back until it appeared somewhat neat and orderly.

A branch snapped close by. She stopped mid-lick of her paw and trained her gaze toward the direction of the sound.

So, her ears weren't deceiving her, after all. She made a quick empathic check on the cubs, ensuring they were still safe, then crouched low to the ground. Lashing her tail about in anticipation, she watched and waited for the slightest movement. She released a low warning growl, hoping whoever or whatever was hiding would have second thoughts about staying any longer. After a few moments of no activity, however, Cammy took the initiative. She slinked toward the direction of where she'd heard the sound last, which led her to a wide trunk of a large tree. She sniffed again, and this time she caught something interesting.

Something… familiar.

Narrowing her eyes, she inched closer to the tree. Then she stopped, dug her claws into the dirt and lowered her body farther into a pouncing position.

A shadow appeared and disappeared with catlike speed. Cammy's heart pounded. *What in the—*

In a blink, a great weight suddenly tackled her to the ground. Her body jostled and the world spun as she tried to retaliate. Her back slammed against the ground, knocking the wind out of her. She blacked out a moment. Finally, she was subdued, her front and back paws pinned down by a heavy weight.

Cammy slowly opened her eyes. Another tiger, its fur covered in mud and leaves, stared back at her with its dark, brooding eyes and snarled.

She widened her eyes. Then her look of initial shock morphed to disgust and rage, and she projected a telepathic message to the other tiger.

"Hello, Furball."

THE END

About the Author

MARIE LONG is a novelist who enjoys the snowy weather, the mountains, and a cup of hot white chocolate. She's an avid supporter of literacy movements. To learn more about her, visit her website: www.marielongauthor.com.

www.ingramcontent.com/pod-product-compliance
Lightning Source LLC
Chambersburg PA
CBHW030817210726
48290CB00002B/638